PENGUIN BOOKS

NANA

Delacorta is the pen name of Daniel Odier, a young Swiss novelist and screenwriter, about whom Anaïs Nin once wrote, 'He is an outstanding writer and a dazzling poet.'

Born in Geneva in 1945, Daniel Odier studied painting in Rome, received his university degree in Paris, and worked as a music critic for a leading Swiss newspaper before taking off for a tour of Asia which culminated in a book on Taoism. His first book, *The Job: Interviews with William Burroughs*, was published in the United States in 1969. Since then, he has published seven novels in France under his real name, two of which have become the bases for films: *Light Years Away* by director Alain Tanner, and *Broken Dreams*, which will be directed by John Boorman. As 'Delacorta' he has written four books, *Diva*, *Nana*, *Luna* and *Lola*; the first has been made into the hit film *Diva* and the last into a film by French national television.

D0544035

DELACORTA

NANA

a novel

TRANSLATED BY VICTORIA REITER

PENGUIN BOOKS

Penguin Books Ltd, Harmondsworth, Middlesex, England
Penguin Books, 40 West 23rd Street, New York, New York 10010, U.S.A.
Penguin Books Australia Ltd, Ringwood, Victoria, Australia
Penguin Books Canada Ltd, 2801 John Street, Markham, Ontario, Canada L3R 1B4
Penguin Books (N.Z.) Ltd, 182–190 Wairau Road, Auckland 10, New Zealand

First published in France 1979
This translation published in the USA by Summit Books 1984
Published in Great Britain by Allen Lane 1984
Published in Penguin Books 1985

Made and printed in Great Britain by
Richard Clay (The Chaucer Press) Ltd, Bungay, Suffolk

FOR EMILE Z.

CHAPTER

1

IT DID NOT RESEMBLE A TRI-
umph of modern technology, but rather looked more like a
child's toy left outside to rust. The depot seemed abandoned and a hobo jungle had taken root in a line of freight
cars parked on a siding. A tin-roofed building slid slowly
into view and the train wheels screeched to a stop, un-
greased brakes squealing. Serge Gorodish, the last passenger
off the train, left the end car and walked the entire length of
the platform toward the ugly cement station building.

He was tall, his face almost Oriental in feature, with eyes
as black as tunnels and a faint scar on the dark amber skin
just beneath his left eye. There was something avid about
his mouth, which was held in a small, fixed smile, a clear
warning that this man was dangerous when provoked. He
moved gracefully, his gestures large and slow, as if he was
used to giving things time to happen. Like his massive but
delicate hands, the battered gray Samsonite suitcase he carried had seen heavy use. It looked as if a tiger had sharpened
his claws on it. Gorodish wore a suit of gray tweed flecked
with black. It, too, had seen some use.

Serge Gorodish pushed through the swinging glass doors and into a waiting room. It smelled of stale cigarette smoke, Gauloises, Royal Menthol and Pall Mall; and of sweat and the tang of radiator-warmed travel posters inviting tourists to savor the beauty of the French provinces.

The waiting room held a couple and a lone man seated on a bench. A dog sniffed at a trash can while a young blond girl, about thirteen years old, petted it. The man on the bench called out: "Alba, leave that dog alone and come sit down."

She turned and Gorodish saw her face. A connoisseur of the great masters of painting, he immediately compared her to Botticelli's Venus stepping from a seashell. Then, after a few seconds, Gorodish forgot about Botticelli. Alba's blond beauty, her youth, her pale skin, overshadowed the remembered image. The fire in her eyes was enough to burn out the air conditioning in a movie theater, and the way she moved, as she rose, held the promise of paradise. Gorodish had nothing against an occasional voyage to nirvana. He blinked, squinted, trying to break the momentary spell of the girl's beauty, then crossed the waiting room and went out into the street.

The sun was beating down on a town that seemed as rich, quiet and comfortable as a country club brunch. It contained 1 main street, 1 park, 67 stores, 24 factories and small businesses, 19 cafés, 1 bookshop, 3 hotels, 11 restaurants, 3 banks, 2 high-priced brothels, 3 Catholic churches, 2 call girls who rarely left their apartment, 1 Protestant church, 1 public swimming pool, 1 newspaper, 1 prison.

All this in the service of 12,300 inhabitants (9400 Catholics, 387 Protestants, 6149 leftists, 6151 rightists). No mosque. No more synagogue.

Gorodish walked halfway up the Rue de Gaulle and stopped in front of the Danton, a sidewalk café directly across from the city hall. It looked perfect.

He sat down and ordered a *panaché*, half beer, half lem-

8

onade. Three men in work clothes, their noses red as poppies, were playing cards and finishing off a bottle of Beaujolais. An old woman sat reading a gossip sheet, a blue-point Siamese cat perched on her knees. The sounds of a pinball machine echoed through the open door of the café. Hairy young men hunched over the game, their voices loud as the heavy metal ball skittered and bumped across the plastic, triggering lights in its path. A Lucite blond smiled and gleamed on the scoreboard. Her breasts glowed crimson as the total rose to 525.

Gorodish glanced at his Hong Kong–made Omega wristwatch. It was 4:47 P.M. He drank the *panaché* in one long swallow. The slow intoxication filling him owed nothing to the bittersweet liquid flowing over his tongue. Rather, it was due to that stronger, more explosive mixture named Alba.

Forcing herself to walk slowly, Alba entered the department store. Her legs were weak, her fingers trembled slightly. A tingling feeling rose from her belly to encompass her entire body as her breathing grew shallow. She brushed back her long blond hair and breathed deeply, to settle her nerves. She could feel tremors in the muscles of her narrow buttocks, and the small golden hairs on her arms rose. A halo seemed to shimmer about the displays as she tried to decide what to steal first. When the saleswoman at the perfume counter reached down to find a smaller bottle of "Y" by Yves Saint-Laurent, Alba slid a demonstrator atomizer into her black and gold plastic Nina Ricci handbag.

She spent long minutes in the record department, staring at the salesman. He began to finger his pink tie, inspecting himself in a mirror. Alba opened the black purse and *Weasels Ripped My Flesh* by Frank Zappa and The Mothers of Invention disappeared from sight. She left the record department when the salesman began recombing his hair.

Her fingers plunged into the fine, silky material displayed at the lingerie counter. Quickly, casually, she liberated a pair

9

of underpants and matching bra in Quiana, size 32B, color: flamingo.

Sipping a strawberry milk shake, she rested from her labors in the store's bar, her blue eyes spotting one of the three detectives the store had hired to discourage shoplifters. To her practiced gaze, the man was as inconspicuous as a fly in a bowl of cream.

Gorodish sat admiring the facade of the city hall building.

"It was built in 1730," said a man at a neighboring table. "Never been restored. Impressive, isn't it?"

"The proportions are off. It's a little too tall."

"You're right, you're right, the design's not perfect. You certainly know your architecture."

"I should," Gorodish said. "I put in two years at the Beaux-Arts."

"I knew it, I knew it. I could tell by the way you were studying the building."

"You're very observant."

"Oh, I'm paid to be observant. I'm editor in chief of *The Independent*."

"The local weekly?"

"We're bigger than that, bigger than that; we cover the whole region: 135,000 copies a week. Say, you want another drink?"

"Yes, all right. I'll have a *panaché*."

"François," the man called, "another *panaché*, and a cognac for me."

"This seems like a nice town," Gorodish said. "I've been looking for a quiet place to work on my sketching. You get out of practice, painting nothing but abstracts."

"You have a place to stay?"

"Not yet."

"Try the Hôtel de la Poste, on that first street to your left. A friend of mine runs it. You tell him I sent you. It's nothing fancy but you'll be comfortable there and the food's good. The specialty's frogs' legs. By the way, my name's Luc Plassin."

"Serge Gorodish."

"Russian?"

"My parents were, but I was born in Paris."

"Monsieur Luc," the waiter said, "you finished the last bottle of Remy Martin. Can I bring you something else?"

"Hennessy." The waiter left.

"You look like you could use a drink," Gorodish said.

"With all this heat I need a little pick-me-up around five o'clock," Plassin said. "I put the whole paper to bed by myself. Nobody to help me except an apprentice, and he's not too bright. Couldn't write more than one column inch on anything except football games or rugby matches. If the owner didn't have *me* working for him, it'd be the end of his political career."

"He a senator?"

"No, he's got the itch, but no brains. Name's Robillard. Been mayor here for twenty-two years, thanks to me and my newspaper. Almost got himself elected representative about five years ago but he was being blackmailed and quit while he was ahead. He had a thing going with the little sisters, they're our local ... call girls I guess you'd call them. Not bad-looking, either. They made a nice piece of change with the pictures they had of him. Robillard bought the local château, to make up for the end of his political ambitions, I guess. He made his money in wholesale wines and liquors. Sends me a dozen bottles of old Armagnac every Christmas, the kind you can't find anymore. Drop in at the paper someday and I'll let you have a taste. The office is about a hundred yards back down Rue de Gaulle. You can't miss it: there's a newspaper in the display window out front."

The waiter brought the drinks. Plassin emptied his glass, throwing his head back as he drank. He paid, gave a small wave of his hand and left, stopping at the tobacco counter on his way out to buy two packs of unfiltered Gauloises cigarettes.

Gorodish took out a small red notebook and wrote:

Luc Plassin, about 60, editor of *The Independent.* Underpaid, alcoholic, right-wing, Indochina War (tattoo on left forearm). Uses same whores as his boss. Knows everybody in town. Gestures: checks wristwatch, scratches right earlobe. Lives alone. Easy.

At first the innkeeper was reserved, but the mention of Luc Plassin's name brought smiles and a display of warmth. In the space on the hotel registration card meant for listing his profession, Gorodish wrote: "Painter."

The innkeeper glanced down and said smoothly: "I would have bet you were an artist. . . . Luc knows a lot about art. Well, you'll have all the peace and quiet you need here. I have two rooms free: Number seven at fifteen francs a day, breakfast included, or number twelve at twenty-one francs. It has a private shower and a view of the park. "

"I'll take number twelve."

"Is your luggage at the train station?"

"No. This is all I brought with me."

"I know how it is: artistic folks travel light. If you want to take your meals here I could do a little better on the price. How about sixty francs a day?"

"All right."

"How long did you plan on staying with us?"

"Just a few weeks."

Gorodish placed his suitcase on the bed and opened the window. The park lay before him, as natural and unrestrained as a gathering of diplomats. The city gardeners had evidently been working overtime: the park was filled with reflecting pools, ridiculous small fountains, trees so identical they might have been stamped from a mold.

A table, a chair, a blond wood armoire, a night stand.

12

The door leading to the bathroom. Above the bed, a Bernard Buffet print which Gorodish took down and threw into the armoire. The bell in the city hall tower rang six times. Three minutes later a church bell answered it, a quarter tone higher. The proper separation of Church and State.

At 7:30 Gorodish went down to the restaurant. Small tables with red-checked cloths, the room filled with the sounds of chewing, slurping, swallowing. Gorodish read the menu and then ordered a country pâté, rabbit in mustard sauce, fresh fruit for dessert, and a half bottle of Chiroubles.

After dinner he went out into the street and breathed deeply of the pure night air before setting off to reconnoiter the town.

Blinking red and yellow lights. He moved toward them. A fancy drugstore, a caterwaul of music filling the air. Bright lights, industrial carpeting, and black vinyl upholstery in the coffee-shop booths contrasted sharply with the provincial austerity of the town. The ground floor held newspapers, magazines, books, records, and gadgets of all sorts. A stairway led up to the coffee shop, its floor and walls lined with gray smoked glass. Gorodish bought a copy of *The Independent* and took a table at the balcony's edge. He watched the people below him for a while, then ordered coffee and began to read. After finishing the paper, he pulled a Swiss army knife from his pocket and carefully cut out a picture of the mayor and his wife taken at the official opening of a new community center. He also cut out the schedule of the Palace movie theater. Luchino Visconti's *Senso* was showing at 9:00 P.M.; *Wild Virgins*, rated X, no one under eighteen admitted, was showing at midnight. He clipped out an advertisement for a secondhand upright piano, 450 francs, the photo of the president of a local bicycle factory posing with his one-hundred-thousandth bicycle, the address of the largest used-car lot in town, and an interview with a local doctor strongly opposed to abortion.

Gorodish placed the newspaper cuttings in his inside

jacket pocket and raised the now-cold coffee to his lips. Blond hair caught his eye. "Alba," said a voice in his head. He watched her as she stood at the gadget counter, inspecting a Kodak Instamatic camera, dressed in patchwork jeans and an Indian tunic. She did not notice him. He saw her hesitate, then pull thirteen ten-franc notes from her pocket and hold them out to the salesman, who put the camera in a paper bag and handed it to her. She turned toward the door.

Gorodish watched her go. She disappeared, leaving a luminous afterimage in his mind.

Gorodish sat on the cold, cement stairs, watching the entrance to the Palace movie theater. A dozen evil-looking motorcycle riders drove up, parked their loudly farting bikes in a line at the curb, and strutted across the courtyard toward the movie theater. The bikers wore jeans and long hair. The back of their leather jackets were emblazoned with a red hand and the word: VAMPIRES.

Other customers arrived: two couples, several hunchbacked elderly people, a few very young movie fans who rode up on mopeds. Gorodish memorized the faces as they passed, studying them in the uneven light coming from the store windows surrounding the courtyard.

Inside, the movie began. Naked women strolled beside the columns of a Roman villa. In the distance, a cloud of dust: the hero, his red cape floating in the wind, drew near. Two women embraced. In the darkened theater avid eyes inspected the bodies of the wild virgins. Laughter, and a running commentary, came from the balcony where Vampires perched.

Gorodish sat at the table in front of the open window, breathing in the sweet night air as he sketched the faces of three men in his notebook. He drew a question mark beside each face and then rose from the table and lit the bedside lamp. Turning off the overhead light, he undressed and slid between the cool sheets.

He could hear the cry of a cuckoo, steps on the sidewalk below, the murmur of a radio in a nearby room. He thought he could hear a piano playing and listened intently, recognizing the Beethoven Sonata no. 1, opus 10, wishing he could hear it more clearly.

Gorodish reached down and pulled the suitcase from beneath the bed. Inside was a worn leather briefcase. He opened it and took out a series of 8 x 10 glossies of little girls, photographed in poses that were simultaneously chaste and enticing. He contemplated the undeveloped bodies for several long minutes.

These were his greatest creation, the height of his artistic sensibility, the most profound expression of his genius. His talent for this special art form had been recognized, and rewarded, by collectors all over the world. His creativity had grown, had blossomed and flourished. He had even published a deluxe edition for his most devoted fans: it had sold out before publication and could no longer be bought, for love or money. Then, one day, he had learned that there was a warrant out for his arrest for contributing to the delinquency of a minor.

Gorodish had closed his photography studio and gone back to oil painting, supporting himself with odd jobs. Opportunities to make big money had come his way, but they had all involved subordinating himself to the whims of others. Gorodish had never liked being dependent on others for his livelihood. He had decided to leave Paris and had come to this town, this typical provincial French town. He was here to reorganize his life, to try to see his way more clearly, to discover his true vocation, to found a private industry in which there would be no competition.

It would take time. He had time.

CHAPTER

2

BY EIGHT IN THE MORNING Gorodish was at work in the Rue de Gaulle, drawing the houses that lined the street and making quick pencil sketches of the passersby. He had always found faces more informative than the most elaborately composed résumé. At one time he had worked as a caricaturist for a magazine.

Now he wanted a clear view of the town, its principal points of interest, its leading citizens. His drawings would help set the stage, describe the characters, uncover the secret workings, the hidden passions, in this apparently placid community.

Stores were beginning to open. Housewives appeared, shopping baskets in hand. A white Ford Granada parked nearby and the driver got out of the car. He appeared to be about forty years old and wore a mauve-colored suit and gleaming patent-leather shoes. The man crossed the street and entered a hair-styling salon. It was 9:15 A.M. Five women employees of the salon had arrived a quarter of an hour earlier. Gorodish added a sketch of the resplendent male to the all-female cast he had drawn earlier.

Around ten, the manager of the photo supply store crossed the street and went into the salon. Almost immediately the two men came out again and headed for the tables in front of the Danton café. Gorodish added another face to his page.

A pair of Vampires lounged on their motorcycles, watching Gorodish and snickering. One second's glance and Gorodish had captured them on his sketch pad.

"Hey, Pops, whatchu drawin'?"

Gorodish looked up at them, indifferent.

They roweled their motorcycles to life. As they rode past Gorodish, the smaller Vampire kicked out at him and the sketch pad flew from his hands. The Vampires disappeared around the corner. Calmly, Gorodish bent over and picked up the fallen sketch pad.

"What was the name again?" the secretary demanded nasally.

"Serge Gorodish."

"Do you have an appointment?"

"No."

"Well, I don't think he'll be able to fit you in this morning . . ."

Three minutes later, Plassin and Gorodish walked out the front door of *The Independent* and up the street to the Danton café where they took a table in the shade. The photographer and the hair stylist were nowhere to be seen.

She stood on the sidewalk opposite the café, wearing a short red skirt and yellow blouse. Gorodish knew her face by heart: he did not need to draw it.

"How's the hotel?" Plassin asked.

"Fine. Exactly what I wanted."

"You started work early this morning. I was watching from my office window. Could I see . . ."

"If you like." Gorodish handed him the sketch pad.

"You have a real talent for caricature," Plassin said.

17

"I used to earn my living at it."

"This is incredible! I recognize everybody. . . . Would you like to know who you've drawn?"

"Yes, all right, that might be interesting," Gorodish said.

"This one's Sandro Leonetti. He's a psychoanalyst, been living here for the last two years. Lots of patients. Gave lectures when he first arrived, sort of to introduce himself to the town. Women like him. He charges five hundred francs a session and is booked solid. There's a rumor around that he's married and has two children somewhere in Italy, but I think he lives alone, here in town. Buys a new Porsche every year. Just bought some land and is going to build a house, very contemporary design. Blanquin, the architect, is doing the plans. You don't have Blanquin in your collection. I've heard that Leonetti's hot for some woman here in town, a rich widow, one of his patients. I'd guess it's the woman who runs the bookshop. Knowing her, I don't think he's scored, yet. Leonetti has a manicure every week, at François Puig's place. This girl you've drawn here, Jasmina, does his nails."

"What's this Puig like?"

"Dresses well. He's got these five good-looking girls working for him but I think he likes boys: you know what I mean. He's real close with Da Sallo, the antique dealer . . . they had some trouble about a year ago. They'd organized a swing weekend at Da Sallo's house in the woods, about twenty-five miles outside of town. One of the boys turned out to be a minor, told his parents about it. They threatened to go to the cops if Puig didn't pay up. I heard it cost him a hundred thousand francs to hush it up, and they're not through bleeding him yet. The photographer is married, he's not as obvious as Puig. But he's got his own racket: smuggling cameras in from Singapore and Hong Kong. Sometimes he puts old lenses on new camera bodies. I've also heard that he's involved in the porn trade, selling dirty pictures in Africa."

"You know the girls who work in the salon?"

"No, except for Jasmina. She's been there three years, handles the cash register, and runs the place when Puig's away. She's got her own clientele. Walk-in customers have to settle for one of the other girls."

"Do you go there to get your hair cut?"

"Are you kidding? It's too expensive. A hundred and fifty francs for a cut, seventy-five francs for a shave. But Leonetti's there every morning. Sometimes I think it's the only recreation he gets."

"Who else goes to Jasmina?"

"Marc de Bonneville. Richest man in the region. Owns three factories: bicycles, farm machinery, surgical instruments. Then there's André Magne. He's in real estate. Owned that château that Robillard just bought. A lot of money there. Deals in stolen antiques, sells gentrified slums. Luigi Da Sallo's his partner, restores and furnishes the houses for Magne to sell. Da Sallo has his own deals going in Italy, paintings, you know: unknown eighteenth-century Italian minor masters that nobody ever heard of. Sells them mainly to the American engineers working at the computer research center outside of town."

"Then there's Sylvain Saudan. He owns the drugstore," Plassin said. "I helped organize a protest march when he started building it. Saudan also owns a place called The Cottage. Downstairs it's a high-priced restaurant. Upstairs there's a half-dozen rooms for his associates and their girlfriends. Saudan lives there. It's a whole other world: most of the people come from out of town. Last year he was fined six hundred thousand francs for tax fraud. Bonneau was the judge on the case. He's one of Jasmina's regulars: comes in for a shave every day. I guess those are the most important clients. Oh, there're a few others who splurge from time to time, trying to make people think they can afford it, or that they have clout."

"What about Jasmina?"

"She lives in a studio apartment at the Balzac Apartments, the three-story building in the street behind your hotel. Jasmina makes a very nice living. Actually, she's the one who makes that business go. The girl's money-hungry. Nothing less than a ten-franc tip if you want another appointment. Her latest boyfriend's Daniel Levi, an architect here in town. Designed the Balzac Apartments. He works alone. A real shark."

"Who's this?" Gorodish asked, pointing at the caricature of a man for whom he had felt an instinctive revulsion.

"Paul Ribon. You've really captured the man: a pig. During the war he was responsible for sending several Jewish families to the camps. He was condemned to death after the Liberation but managed to have the sentence commuted and set aside. It's been a long time since I felt any faith in our legal system, but that fellow . . ." Plassin shook his head. "People forget. He's managed to maneuver himself into a job with a private security firm. Wouldn't you know he's the kind of man who talks about law and order?"

"Really?" Gorodish said, knowing himself to be a man who believed in occasionally taking justice into his own hands.

A bell tinkled as she opened the door and entered the variety store. Monsieur Jean, seventy years old and almost deaf, was putting espadrille sandals back in their boxes. She walked up behind him and touched his shoulder. He turned, smiling, his Basque beret perched on his head. The hearing aid hidden in his glasses was obviously not working.

"I have to get a new bell," he shouted, "can't hear a damn thing. What do you want, sweetheart?"

"Papa wants to know if his compressed-air corkscrew came in."

"I think so, but I haven't opened the carton yet. Just a minute."

Monsieur Jean's store held a hodgepodge of merchandise and if the old man did not have an item he always knew where to get it. He began slicing open a carton with a worn Boy Scout knife. Alba edged over to the cash drawer. She opened it slowly, removed six hundred-franc notes and closed it again. Monsieur Jean began to curse. "I don't know where the hell it is. The salesman just left. . . . Tell your daddy I'll have it for him tomorrow. . . ."

After a late-morning aperitif, Gorodish and Plassin lunched at the Hôtel de la Poste restaurant. The chicken fricasse was superb, especially accompanied, as it was, by the full bottle of Vosne-Romanée 1969 that Plassin had insisted on ordering. Plassin was feeling wonderful, full of new energy and self-confidence. It had been a long time since he had been able to speak with someone without seeing visible signs of boredom on the listener's face. Gorodish had brought a measure of adventure into Plassin's boring, solitary life. Gorodish was an artist. Gorodish was intelligent. He listened to Plassin talk with unflagging interest and obvious pleasure.

After a serving of especially pungent Roquefort cheese, a portion of chocolate mousse and coffee, the two men sipped a 1929 Armagnac from Mayor Robillard's own cellars. Gorodish carefully rolled the delicate snifter between his palms, warming the amber liquid with the heat of his hands. He was feeling lucky: he had accomplished months of work in mere days. His collection of portraits was growing, his vision of the mechanisms which kept the town going, kept it functioning peaceably, was becoming clearer. A few, well-placed grains of sand and the entire, delicately balanced machine would grind to a halt.

Gorodish spent the early part of the afternoon setting down everything he had learned, covering seventeen pages in the red notebook with his cramped handwriting. He tore a page from the sketch pad and drew a graph, listing the names of the leading citizens and the number of the page in the red notebook where the proper information could be found. Then he sat for an hour, not moving, his head buried

21

in his hands. At last he looked up, rubbed his eyes, and began drawing lines linking some of the names.

A hot shower refreshed him. A bath towel wrapped around his waist, he lay napping on the bed, dreaming of his childhood. His dead parents. The Paris neighborhood near the Bastille where he was raised. His apprenticeship in a bakery. His piano lessons with Nadia, the old Russian *émigrée* who used to rap him on the head with her cane. The passionate love of music that lasted until his twenty-third year. The odd jobs that kept him alive until the day he was hired to play piano in a bar. His first real paycheck. His two new passions, little girls and sketching, that eventually turned music into nothing more than a means of earning a living. The attempted seductions that failed. The fear of scandal. The long, platonic love affairs. In the beginning, sketching had been merely the excuse he used in order to gaze at those naked young bodies. Then, at some indefinite point he could not recall, the sketching became more important than the bodies. Jean Saporta, a small-time gangster, had taken a liking to him, had offered him a salary large enough to support his passions. The job was simple: Gorodish accompanied Saporta everywhere, driving his sky-blue Chevrolet Impala and occasionally doing him odd favors. Gorodish had become involved with a twenty-three-year-old hooker who, despite her advanced years, earned a good living acting the perverse virgin. During the long hours spent waiting behind the wheel, he had taken to sketching people he saw in the street. Finally he grew tired of taking orders and quit, finding another job almost immediately as a messenger boy for a magazine. One of the reporters noticed his talent for caricature and Gorodish had been promoted, spending the next two years drawing politicians and movie stars.

A dozen motorcycles stood silently before the darkened garage. Inside, the Vampires were celebrating the initiation of Ted, their newest recruit. The only light came from candles stuck in old bottles. A battery-powered tape recorder squawked indecipherable music. Twelve young men and eight girls lolled about on stained mattresses, passing a joint from hand to hand. A black sheet covered the rear wall; someone had sewn a bright red hand on it.

After suffering through three months of savagery, Ted was taking advantage of the rights and privileges of membership in the Vampires by humping two girls at the same time.

The preliminaries to joining the Vampires had been simple enough. He had had the necessary qualifications: he owned a monster cycle with a 350 cc engine, and he had a cooperative girlfriend. For the last three months she had spent all her free time balling anybody who wanted her. Except Ted. He had been kept busy stealing whatever he was ordered to steal: a car in broad daylight, five hundred francs which he had turned over to the gang.

And he had survived the manhunt. It had taken place in the forest outside town. Ted had been the prey; the Vampires, the hunters. The rules afforded him only a one-minute head start, but Ted had managed to evade them for an entire night. After that he had spent a full week locked in the garage without food, without light. At the end of the week he had been branded on the left shoulder and then had allowed himself to be worked over by every member of the gang. The initiation had ended after Ted had submitted himself to whatever further humiliations the Vampires had been able to invent.

Most candidates did not make it. The weak point was often the girl. She had to prove her worth, and his, by screwing whoever wanted her, whenever he wanted her. She was expected to steal clothing from a town resident chosen at random by the Vampires, to submit to being whipped and branded, and to take part in various other diversions and exercises. If she flinched she was out, but the candidate was given a chance to make up for her weakness with another girl, if he could find someone suitable, and willing.

Ted and his girlfriend had survived the three months of torture and were now full-fledged Vampires, free to do as they pleased, equal to the others. The town's teenagers knew all about the initiation rites, and the Vampires were envied, feared and admired.

Freddie crushed the saliva-wet roach against a paint-can lid. The Vampires were in the process of painting the clubhouse walls black. "You seen that new guy in town?"

"The one's always drawin' somethin'?"

"Yeah. They don' like him aroun'. I been hearin' things, people wonderin' what the hell he's doin' here."

"He's nothin'."

"Maybe we could use him."

"How?"

"Well, suppose we was to pull off somethin', we could maybe do it so they'd blame him, right? But we'd havta do it real smart."

"Yeah."

"Yeah. We been gettin' soft, jus' sittin' aroun'."

"Yeah. You got somethin' in mind, right?"

"Yeah. Somethin'. If we do it right we wouldn' havta worry about money. . . ."

"Whatchur plan?"

"Le's say we got four of us inside, and two on the outside, and the rest set up to kinda keep people's minds offa what we're doin'. . . ."

After dinner Gorodish spent an hour at a table in front of the Danton, drinking coffee and listening to conversations, watching faces, studying attitudes. He was waiting for Alba to put in her nightly appearance, but she had not come. He realized that he knew nothing about her. Yet it would have been easy enough: he could have waited for her outside the school and followed her home. Three women stared at him insistently, although he was about as physically attractive as

24

a dump truck. Gorodish spotted Sylvain Saudan, the drug-store's owner, driving past in a black Mercedes.

Determined to forget about his plan for just one evening, Gorodish left the Danton and strolled through the town. The drugstore was as busy as ever. No Alba. He walked on. He had an appointment at ten with the ladies responsible for putting an end to Mayor Robillard's political career: they could probably teach him more about the town than old Plassin had.

The sisters lived on the eighth floor of a luxury apartment building. The lobby was swathed in marble. The walls were mirrored and green plants decorated the entryway. Gorodish inspected himself approvingly in the mirrored wall of the elevator. He pressed the doorbell button. It sounded a major third interval: E-flat, G-natural. A good omen.

They were beautiful: one blond, one brunette. They offered him a gin and tonic, the heat, isn't it just terrible? They wore matching green silk Chinese robes and were fascinated by his refreshingly intelligent conversation. Oh, it was such a bore seeing the same old faces all the time, those old men, those dull heavy-hitters, the occasional sexually clumsy teenager. They invited him to step into the dressing room and change into something more comfortable. The bed was covered with black satin sheets.

Passionately, their hearts beating wildly, they caressed the firm muscles of his overwhelmingly virile body, the heat rising from the center of their being to meet the challenge of his furious lust.

Actually: the walls were lacquered midnight blue. Rococo, gilt-framed mirrors faced the bed. The three bodies reflected in the mirrors moved slowly at first, then faster. Spotlights sculpted abstract forms onto the melded, blending flesh. Gorodish thought of Alba, trying to hold her firmly in his mind, the fantasy crippled by the double image, the sexual parenthesis formed by the women's bodies on either side of him.

CHAPTER

3

A MONTH PASSED AS GORO-
dish explored the town, trying to discover its hidden pat-
terns, his painstaking observation uncovering secret rivalries,
latent tensions. Under its apparently peaceful exterior the
town was a sleeping volcano.

Gorodish made plans for the second phase of the opera-
tion: forcing the currents of antagonism and hatred to the
surface. After which, he would sit back and wait for the explosion.

On one of his long walks through the area, he discovered
a small, isolated cabin in the woods about twenty minutes
from town. The cabin belonged to a local gamekeeper who,
seeing Gorodish's interest, offered to rent it to him for two
hundred francs a month. The key safely in his pocket,
Gorodish rationalized the move on the grounds of better
understanding the town by distancing himself from it. He
moved in the next day.

The cabin smelled slightly of mildew and a beam of sunlight filtered through one warped shutter. Gorodish opened
the windows and the sun came streaming into the room, re-

vealing its spare furnishings: a double bed, a table, four chairs, a sink, a small woodburning stove, pots, three glasses, two plates, silverware. The cabin was equipped with running water, but no electricity. Two lamps stood on the table. Gorodish shook them. He would have to buy kerosene.

Logs lay piled to one side of the blackened, soot-filled fireplace. He found old newspapers and some pinecones in the woodbox, and started a fire, hoping it would help rid the cabin of its dampness.

He made a list of what was needed to make the cabin habitable. There were pillows and blankets on the bed and the gamekeeper had told him where to find firewood. He would buy sheets, kerosene for the lamps, matches, a small ax for chopping kindling, dishwashing detergent, and food staples. The idea of cooking for himself was appealing: Gorodish was tired of restaurant meals. Smoke hung in the air. He pushed the logs deeper into the fireplace with a pair of tongs.

Gorodish spent the afternoon in town, shopping. A grocer agreed to deliver his order to the road near the cabin; Gorodish would have to carry the cartons the rest of the way up the forest path.

Several of the town children trooped after him as he went from store to store. Gorodish's popularity had begun with the appearance of a feature article in *The Independent*. Titled "Portrait of an Artist," Plassin's article had turned shopkeepers conciliatory and caused the townspeople to greet him as he sat at his table in front of the Danton, or when passing him on the street. Mothers encouraged their children to watch the artist at his work: a sketch might fall their way. Gorodish enjoyed the children. Talking with them taught him much about the town. Plassin's article had called Gorodish "an artist of great talent." Plassin had merely misinterpreted where Gorodish's true genius lay.

The wine bottles lay in a neat row beneath the sink. Sugar, salt, pepper, coffee, bread, and honey stood on shelves; the rest of the provisions were in a wall cupboard. A clean odor of burning wood crept through the room. His notes and sketches waited on the table.

Gorodish lay on the newly made bed. He had compiled dossiers on eighty-five of the town's leading citizens, searching out the proper antagonist, the perfect adversary, for each one. He had discovered the secret shames, the private dishonors, the lines of hatred binding the people of the town. By projecting the effect of various combinations and juxtapositions, Gorodish was able to foretell exactly who would be suspect in each case.

Cheap, untraceable stationery and fifty-centime stamps lay next to his notebook. The lamps held enough kerosene to last until dawn. There was nothing left for him to do now but write the letters exposing secrets the town had thought buried forever. Yet, Gorodish hesitated. It seemed to him that nightfall would be a more appropriate time to begin his work.

Alba glanced at the Bulova Accutron watch an American tourist had left on the dashboard of his rented, metallic green Citroën sedan.

It was three in the morning and, even with the uncurtained window open, the attic bedroom was oppressively hot. Alba lay naked on the bed, staring out at the sky, the moon playing on her body, its milky light wavering with each breath she took. On the floor below her father, older sister, and younger brothers slept. Her mother was ill, so her father said, being cared for in a convalescent hospital. Alba knew the truth: her mother had run away with another man. Alba had overheard her father on the telephone, begging his wife to come back. Afterward, he had begun drinking again. This attic room was Alba's sanctuary from the real world, a place where she could daydream and act out her fantasies.

She opened the top drawer of the dresser, the drawer she called "the treasure chest." It was filled with plunder from

28

her expeditions through the town stores: expensive lingerie, money, watches, bottles of perfume, gold pens, cigarette lighters, silk scarves, rings, necklaces. The sight filled her with joy. Alba lit a candle fixed in a saucer. The flame sputtered and rose, illuminating her naked body silhouetted against the darkened bedroom walls. She stared at her reflection in the high mirror over the dresser. A small breeze caressed her skin. She found a pair of black silk stockings in the drawer and slowly drew them on, attaching them to a black satin garter belt. A car drove past the house, its tires thudding against the cobblestones. Then the night was silent again. Alba discarded the matching brassiere: she wanted to watch her breasts.

Taking a long, red silk scarf, she twisted it loosely and slipped it between her thighs. Holding tightly to the ends of the scarf she began drawing it back and forth. Her hips began to move. Watching herself in the mirror, Alba thought she looked very, very beautiful.

The motorcycles were too noisy so Freddie and Ted walked through the deserted streets, the weight of the gas can balanced between them. The Vampires knew the artist was living somewhere outside town, but they did not know exactly where. No matter: they were in no hurry. What counted now were the first intimations of disorder, the beginnings of fear spreading through the population. Then, a word dropped here and there, and suspicion would focus on the painter: the dumb chump should have settled somewhere else.

Freddie and Ted listened to the quiet, tensed for the first sign of trouble.

"You gotta cigarette?"

"Asshole, you know what we're carryin'."

"I forgot. Listen, Freddie, I wanna go with you, after. Somebody comes after us we'd have a better chance . . ."

"The plans'r every man for hisself. Smarter tha' way. . . ."

"Don'tcha wanna hang aroun' an' watch?"

"Yeah, but you gotta choose: doin' or watchin'. . . ."

"When I thinka alla assholes who're gonna see it, an' we can't."

"We get outta here in one piece, we can take it easy for a while. . . ."

Fourteen cars sat in the city hall parking lot, one of them a yellow Lotus. At any other time they would have joyfully stolen it. Three of the cars were unlocked. Freddie uncapped the jerrican, wet down the front seats and splashed gasoline around the tires. The gasoline formed a small, greenish puddle between the cars. He dropped a handful of cotton waste into the spilled gasoline and unrolled a length of primer cord. Ted bent over, a lighted match in his hand.

They ran in opposite directions. Four seconds later a blast of air shook the parking lot. An explosion followed. Windows in the city hall disintegrated, shards of glass sliding down to the street. A red light rose in the sky as faces appeared in windows around the square. An alarm rang out. Three minutes later, the first fire engines arrived.

Alone, surrounded by the night cries of forest animals, Gorodish worked on. When dawn broke he brewed a pot of coffee and, cup in hand, came out onto the cabin porch to watch the forest come awake. Unabated, the summer heat seeped down through the leaves and branches of the trees. Gorodish felt strangely serene, filled with a sense of accomplishment. All that remained now was to address and stamp the envelopes.

Gorodish walked up the Rue de Gaulle under the deep, summer-blue sky, stopping briefly at mailboxes along the way. A crowd was gathered in front of the city hall, people standing in animated conversation around several burned-out automobiles. Plassin was busy shooting photos of the cars. He spotted Gorodish and made his way toward him.

30

"You want to get a cup of coffee at the Danton?" Plassin asked.

"I was on my way there," Gorodish replied.

"It's incredible," Plassin said, "the first time anything like this has happened."

"An accident?"

"No. The police found a gas can and a box of matches. Whoever set the fire used primer cord. Didn't you hear the explosion?"

"What time was it?"

"Three-thirty in the morning."

"I was asleep. It would have taken a freight train to wake me."

They found a free table in the sun. "I had a telephone call this morning," Plassin said, seeming amused. "From a woman, or maybe it was a girl. Anyway, she said she saw you around three-fifteen this morning, carrying a gas can up the Rue de Gaulle. Her description of the gas can matched the one the police found."

"Very funny," Gorodish said. "How old was she?"

"I don't know. Young. I guess. She telephoned the police, too. The commissaire knows we're friends, so he called to tell me about it. He isn't taking it too seriously. It was obviously a crank call, she wouldn't give her name, but I thought you ought to know. It looks like you've made yourself some enemies in town. It's natural, of course: you're a stranger here."

"Nothing surprises me anymore."

"Oh, by the way, I saw a Citroën station wagon at the used-car lot, you know, the big one on the left as you come into town? It looked like it's in pretty good shape."

"How much do they want for it?"

"Thirty-two hundred francs."

"How many miles on the odometer?"

"Fifty thousand."

   • • •

31

Despite an active, and thoroughly exhilarating night, Sylvain Saudan was not in a good mood. The new salesgirl he had hired for the drugstore had proved to be an athletic lay, but she was clumsy. The idiot had dropped a large bottle of bath oil into the tub. Saudan liked exotic perfumes when used in moderation, but right now he stank of lotus.

The girl sat across from him, draped in a lilac-colored bath sheet. As Saudan tied the belt on his camel hair bathrobe, there came a soft knock at the door and the butler entered, carrying a heavily laden breakfast tray. He placed the tray on a glass-topped table and bowed his way out of the room. The girl seemed impressed. The tray held a crystal tumbler of orange juice, a fresh pineapple, two three-and-three-quarter-minute eggs, toast, English marmalade, butter and lapsang souchong tea. Saudan was renowned for his refined tastes: he had the tea mailed from Harrods each month to ensure its freshness. That sort of refinement and attention to detail cost his clients a bundle each time they took advantage of the facilities at The Cottage.

The staff at The Cottage was chosen for its efficiency and discretion. If it happened, as it often did, that three or four couples found themselves sharing the room known as "The Rustic Suite," it was with the sure knowledge that their little peccadilloes would be kept secret.

Saudan savored the delicate aroma rising from his teacup. There was a strong possibility that the girl in the lilac towel was broad-minded enough to take part in one of his frequent swing weekends. Saudan contemplated the blue Wedgwood tea service with mixed feelings. Luigi Da Sallo had definitely overcharged him for it.

The girl let the towel slip to her waist. Saudan smiled in appreciation of the gesture and bit into a piece of toast smeared with butter and a layer of marmalade. The girl dropped three sugar cubes into her teacup. Saudan frowned. It suddenly occurred to him that her eyes were the same dull blue as the Wedgwood. Ah, well, perfection was an almost unattainable goal. And he would stink like a gigolo all day due to her carelessness. Of course, there had been moments, during the long, acrobatic night, when he had actually driven the girl out of her mind. Perhaps her matutinal stupidity was simply the aftereffect of his prowess. . . .

"Do you want my egg, darling?" she asked.

"No, thank you. I only eat one."

"I can't eat eggs in the morning." She arranged the towel around her waist. "What time do you want to meet, tonight?"

"One should not overindulge," Saudan said. "It dulls the senses. Let's wait a few days, my dear." Automatically, his hand reached over to dandle her breast, taking care not to upset the teapot. The girl had lovely skin.

The butler appeared again, bringing Saudan's morning mail on a silver tray. A cheap yellow envelope lay on top of the pile. None of Saudan's acquaintances used such shoddy stationery: it was undoubtedly an advertising circular from a local butcher, or wine merchant, or pastry shop. He leaned over to see the return address and was surprised to find that his name had been written by hand. Strange. He opened the envelope with an engraved silver dagger and began to read.

Saudan had received anonymous letters before this. He knew that small towns were filled with envious, bitter people and that, unlike in a big city, it was impossible to hide wealth under a veil of anonymity. But this was not the usual crank letter. This was serious.

The contents of the letter were too pointed, too precise, to have been written by a stranger. He would have to discover which of his friends had sent it and put a stop to the blackmail immediately. No scruples had stood in Saudan's way during his climb to the top. He would not hesitate to do what was necessary to preserve his hard-won position.

Gorodish pressed the accelerator. The Citroën responded well but the brakes felt as if they had been gnawed by rats.

"The original owner took very good care of the car," the salesman said. "He's a personal friend of mine. He washed it every week and kept it polished. The way he took care of it I thought he'd never buy a new one."

"Your friend must be the nervous type," Gorodish said. "He rode the brakes."

"Well, maybe they are a little low. I'll tell you what, if you pay cash I'll throw in a new master cylinder."

"I wouldn't give you more than three thousand for this wreck."

"You've got yourself a deal."

"I want a side-view mirror, too. . . ."

"Keep asking for replacement parts, I might as well sell you a new car."

André Martin, fifty-seven years old, professor of French literature, was known to his students as "Old Decadence" due to his fidelity to the memory of Charles de Gaulle and his taste for outdated and emphatic turns of phrase. Imbued with the importance of his responsibilities as a teacher, he strode up and down before the class, a worn, cardboard notebook in one hand.

His eyes met Alba's. The girl was not without intelligence. She was attractive. He coughed to counteract the sudden warmth in his groin and said loudly:

"Ladies and gentlemen, we come now to the subject of today's essay. You will have three hours in which to display your erudition in a dense, well-reasoned, and gracefully stated analysis of the following dialogue, taken from the pages of *Emile*, and written, I need not remind you, by that most glorious of French philosophers: Jean-Jacques Rousseau. And I quote:

  'Are you young or old?
  'I am young.
  'Is your grandmother young or old?
  'She is old.

'*Was she ever young?*
'*Yes.*
'*Why is she no longer young?*
'*Because she grew old.*'
End of quotation. To repeat . . ."

Gorodish parked the station wagon in front of the *lycée* just as the students came pouring through the doors. He saw Alba. She was wearing jeans and a red cotton T-shirt with COLUMBIA UNIVERSITY printed on the front. A torrent of emotion rose within him. Waiting until she had moved far enough up the street, he began to follow her.

On the way home Alba wondered where she could steal some colored marking pens. They would give her something to do next time Old Decadence inflicted his well-chosen and meaningful essay questions on the class.

The Vampires went into the public-relations business. At noon on Thursday, pairs of bikers appeared in the main cafés in town, talking loudly as they discussed the parking lot explosion. It was probably some nut from the mental hospital outside town. Remember, last summer, that manic-depressive got away and pissed on a cake in the pastry shop window? What about that guy, the one around town always scribbling on a note pad or drawing something, where did he come from? Maybe he did it. There's something funny about that guy. The police found a gas can, proves it wasn't no accident. Etc.

Between ten in the morning and noon, three fistfights broke out between perfectly ordinary, heretofore honorable citizens. Two of the fights caused no appreciable damage: bystanders separated the pugilists before any harm was done. The third fight proved more serious. One of the men was now in the hospital where doctors were attempting to rebuild his face. He had been grossly disfigured by the jagged edge of a broken beer bottle.

Commissaire Leblond was a peace-loving man. In the last few months the men under his command had done nothing more exciting than direct traffic, help kindergarten children cross the street, and shove parking tickets under windshield wipers. The last act of violence had occurred at Christmas, during a confrontation between an unfaithful wife and her classically cuckolded husband, when a police officer had been severely mauled by the adultress in question.

This morning Leblond had been wakened by the explosion but had chosen to remain in bed, considering it a matter for the fire department. Now, however, there had been three public disturbances, one of which looked like it might cause problems for the police.

The guilty party sat before him on a straight-backed chair. The perpetrator was not in handcuffs: he and Leblond were cosponsors of the local rugby team.

André Magne was well-liked. He was wealthy, formerly one of the major vegetable wholesalers in the region, now a real-estate developer. Leblond lit his fifteenth Robert Burns Cigarillo of the day. It was the only brand he could afford that still tasted something like a cigar.

"Have a cigar, André. It's good for the nerves."

"No, thank you."

"What the hell got into you?"

"I can't talk about it."

"You'll have to, if you want me to help. You can trust me, André. Believe me, in the years I've been on the force I've heard just about every story . . ."

"I went crazy."

"What did he do to set you off?"

"I can't tell you."

"Is it something about your wife?"

"My wife? Oh. No. I know she hasn't always been faithful to me, but . . ."

"Talk to me, for God's sake! He's going to sue you when he gets out of the hospital! And he has witnesses. You could wind up in prison."

"I know."

"We've been friends a long time, André. I know you. You're no street brawler. Why can't you tell me? . . ."

Three hours later André Magne was still seated in the straight-backed chair and a frustrated Commissaire Leblond had learned nothing. Except that his friend was afraid of something much worse than prison, or a fine.

Magne was weeping. Everything in the letter was true. The blackmailer had not asked for money, yet, but Magne knew that once he began paying he would never be let off the hook.

What Magne did not know was that he was just one of eighty-five people with the same problem.

CHAPTER

4

THE NORTON 750 CC CHOPPER drifted down a country road, its engine burbling gently in the summer night. Before leaving town, Josephine had twisted Filo's hair into a long braid that dangled down his back, its ends almost touching the heavy leather belt at his waist.

Some of their best times together had been spent like this, far from the gang, riding around for hours on the bike. When there was a full moon Filo did not even bother to turn on the Norton's double iodine-quartz headlights. Oh, they'd had some killer nights.

Josephine was one tough lady. Filo often thought of the initiation they'd suffered through together. He remembered the way she'd looked at him when they'd been branded: he'd screamed louder than she had. If she hadn't been looking straight into his eyes he'd probably have passed out.

But he'd taught her stuff, too: how to use a knife. He'd learned the fine points of knife fighting from an Arab buddy. And how to use a straight razor, and the subtleties of taped razor blades held between the fingers or hidden in the mouth.

Josephine loosened her hold on his waist. Kissing the nape of his neck, she leaned back and stripped off her T-shirt. She loved the feel of the wind on her bare breasts. Filo let go of the raked left handlebar. Josephine helped him remove his jacket and shoved it into the saddlebag. They rode on, Josephine's naked breasts pressing against his back.

After a while, Filo told her to move up front. They'd gone through the routine many times before: Filo bent forward and Josephine crawled over his head. He straightened and she turned to face him, her legs circling his waist. She lay back against the gas tank, her head resting on the speedometer, her back arching. The moon caressed her breasts and her long hair blew forward, tendrils tickling his arms. She loved watching him drive, his body held straight, his arms tensed, hands gripping the ape-hanger handlebars, a serious expression on his face, his long hair pulled back and braided. Jeez, whatta hunk.

Her hands trailed across the muscles of his abdomen, feeling the softness of his skin. She unbuckled the heavy belt and zipped open his pants. Josephine had found a way for them to make love on the motorcycle, replacing the normal zipper on their jeans with another, longer one that ran the full length of the crotch seam. Neither one of them wore underwear.

Josephine unzipped her own jeans. Rising up on the pedals, Filo slowly penetrated her. She moaned, her small mewlings whipped away by the wind. A pale-feathered owl soared far above Filo's head. The motorcycle rolled slowly down the road, Filo standing on the pedals, absolutely still. The vibration from the engine was enough.

The headlights clicked on, splashing yellow against the black asphalt road, the white dividing line seeming to stretch to infinity. Filo shifted into second gear. The cycle roared forward and he rose to his full height, sliding deeper into her. He shifted into third, into fourth. Josephine began to howl. The motor roared as the chopper took three long curves, Filo leaning into them before aiming the cycle down the endless straightaway. They must have been doing a hundred miles an hour when he felt Josephine's spasms begin. Filo closed his eyes. They came at the same time, their rising cries a duet accompanied by the music of the engine revving as high as it could go.

Filo slowed the cycle to its normal cruising speed and dimmed the headlights again. Their shadows stretched out before them, projected onto the road by the lights of an almost silent automobile driving up behind them. Luxury car, Filo thought. They did not move, not caring if they were seen, happy to shock whoever was in the car.

A white Jaguar matched speed with them for a few seconds, four weird women laughing madly behind the car's closed windows. Bizarre, carnival makeup; grins accentuated by painted scarlet mouths; jerky gestures.

"Faggots in drag," Filo shouted.

They watched the Jaguar's rear lights become small red dots, then disappear, the car moving as silently as a sailboat skimming the sea. Too bad you can't hear the motor, Filo thought.

Josephine's back began to ache. She closed both zippers and crawled back over Filo to the tandem seat. He wondered where the fags in the Jag were heading: the car had a Paris license plate. Headlights still dimmed, he pushed the Norton until they could see the car ahead of them, following it, holding back so that they would not be spotted. Ten minutes later the Jaguar turned off onto a side road and drove up to a large white gate. The gate was open. The Jaguar drove through and up a driveway bordered by cypress trees.

The house was enormous. Lights from the ground-floor windows shone on a large, paved courtyard decorated with four larger-than-life statues of Venus.

"We oughta tell the guys," Filo said. "Looks like they're gonna party."

"Le's go get 'em," Josephine agreed. "They wouldn' wanna miss this."

The Misses Adelaide Tronchet, Germaine Titien, and Christine Oloff, professors of piano, solfeggio, and music theory, owners and proprietors of the Children's Conservatory of Music, promoted the annual piano recital by advertising in *The Independent* and placing handpainted cardboard posters in display windows around town. This year the recital was being held in the community center. The usual crowd was in attendance: relatives come to admire the family prodigy, local music lovers, and the curious. Gorodish was one of the latter.

Evidently the professors of piano were not in business solely for their love of music: Gorodish paid his five francs at the door and, wanting legroom, seated himself in the front row. He cast an educated eye on the piano. It was a Pleyel Grand, Model D, built at the turn of the century. He wondered how much tone it had left.

By intermission he was convinced there would be no miracles. The piano sounded terrible. All the recitalists had displayed the same mannerisms: pained expressions, a heavy foot on the pedals, and hands pounding the keys.

Two of the professors were dressed conservatively in black skirts and blouses, their hair pulled back in chignons. The third woman, a round, dumpy bundle of nerves not a day younger than seventy-two and still spry, seemed to have patterned herself on Isadora Duncan. Thin, straggly hair tortured into puffs framed an aging doll's face as withered and shrunken as a dried-out apple. Her formal gown of purple tulle and reembroidered lace harked back to the days of the Great Depression.

Christine Oloff ran the school with an iron hand. She was the only one of the professors to have enjoyed the semblance of a concert career. Readers of *The Independent* were reminded of her triumph at the Salle Gaveau concert hall in

41

Paris, in 1932. But the concert stage had proved too strenuous for her fragile health. After that one recital, Professor Oloff had retired, to devote her life to teaching. Her visiting cards read VIRTUOSO PIANIST.

Gorodish watched as the last student sat down at the piano. His interest was piqued as the boy, who could not have been more than twelve years old, waited for the audience to quiet before beginning. Glancing at the mimeographed program, Gorodish saw that the kid was going to play *Kreisleriana,* by Schumann. The boy was chubby, with a grave expression on his face and perfect pianists' hands: small, with short, powerful fingers. He began.

For the first time that evening Gorodish could hear the piano's true tone. The boy kept on the beat, his nervousness translating itself into just the right amount of power in his touch. There was even a hint of madness in his style. No doubt about it: the kid had talent. Gorodish waited eagerly for the high D at the beginning of the first movement. It was a killer: even the greatest concert pianists occasionally skipped it. The kid hit an E. Already a pro, he hid the sour note in an appoggiatura. In the second part of the first movement he used a little too much pedal during the passage in G-flat, transforming the line into an unneeded sostenuto. He played the rest of the movement superbly, but Gorodish had been trained by a perfectionist. If he had played the beginning that sloppily, Nadia would have hit him with her cane.

The second movement lacked legato, and the kid was not quite in control of his fourth and fifth fingers during the series of octave breaks, but the counterpoint was so well developed that, for a moment, Gorodish thought he was hearing four hands on the keyboard. The brat was a real artist.

Applause. A tear ran down Gorodish's cheek as he shouted "Bravo!" Christine Oloff rewarded him with a smile. She knew a connoisseur when she saw one.

Ululating like an Apache in a Hollywood Western, Filo led the pack of Vampires down the road, all nine choppers purring loudly in the night.

Reaching the private road, they left the choppers in a stand of trees and walked up to the house, keeping to the neatly mowed lawn and avoiding the gravel driveway that might have given them away.

Music came from the brightly lit house. A spotlight hanging in a weeping willow shone down on three cars parked in the courtyard.

They circled the house, taking cover behind trees and flowering bushes. Through open French doors they could see the living room and the flagstone-paved terrace beyond it. A lighted swimming pool formed a bright turquoise patch in the dark.

Two couples were dancing. A third couple lounged on a honey-colored suede sofa, drinking champagne from crystal glasses. Freddie recognized two of the men: François Puig, owner of the hair salon, and Luigi Da Sallo, the antique dealer. They seemed to be enjoying themselves. Da Sallo was playing suckface with one of the drag queens. Disgusting.

Freddie held up his hand and the Vampires slithered back into the undergrowth. "The keys are inna Jaguar," Josephine said. "Us girls could maybe drop in on 'em. Just to scare 'em a little."

"Not bad," Freddie admitted. "We'll watch from here. Jus' make sure nobody gets to a phone."

"Look out for the wop," Filo warned. "He's a kind gotta gun in a drawer someplace. . . ."

"Don' worry," Josephine said, taking out the razor Filo had given her for her birthday. The handle was mother-of-pearl, the blade the finest damascened Solingen steel. She had not used it yet, but it would cut through wood with one flick of her wrist.

"I don' think the car'll get through tha door," Freddie said.

"Don' worry, it'll make it," Josephine assured him. The girls climbed into the Jaguar. It smelled of new leather. They closed the doors quietly, even though the music coming from the house was loud enough to cover the sound. Josephine let the car roll across the courtyard and onto the lawn. She drove carefully around the pool and aimed for the French doors, imagining the Vampires waiting on the far side of the house, imagining them laughing in anticipation.

Through the tinted-glass windshield she saw panic in the men's faces as the Jaguar crashed into the room, overturning a Louis XV pedestal table. A Saxony porcelain vase fell to the floor, its decorative medallion smashing as it hit. Puig's mouth dropped open and the Cuban cigar he had been smoking fell into his lap. The Jaguar came to a stop on the salmon-colored carpet. The girls piled out to stand next to it, smiling hugely.

"How dare you intrude . . ." Luigi Da Sallo gasped.

"Stuff it, Pizza Queen," one of the girls replied.

The transvestites were obviously frightened. "We're being mugged. . . ." one of them screamed.

"You could have scratched that absolutely priceless piece of . . ."

"Save it," said Lola, a big-breasted brunette.

Puig was the first to regain a measure of self-control. "Young ladies, this has been a most amusing interlude. I presume you will join us in a glass of champagne before leaving. . . ."

"Shut your hole, Miss Blow Dry," Josephine said, "an' siddown if you don' wan' 'em cut off."

Da Sallo edged toward the desk, moving as stealthily as a cat backing away from something nasty. He felt a burning sensation on his cheek, glimpsed the red-and-blue design on the blade, and froze, all thought wiped from his mind.

"Take it easy, ladies," Josephine said, "we're runnin' this party now."

His knees trembling, Puig lowered himself into a chair. Da Sallo swabbed at the blood on his face with a handmade Normandy lace handkerchief. One of the girls picked up a bottle of Veuve Cliquot champagne and emptied it over a man in drag, swamping his hairdo. The man made a sound, of fear or pleasure: it was hard to tell.

"There are limits ..." Da Sallo whispered indignantly.

"Insteada runnin' your mouth, whynt you change the record?" Da Sallo obediently changed the record.

Lola gently pushed a Sèvres porcelain coffeepot off the table. It broke quietly, discreetly, on the rug. Nobody said a word.

Da Sallo moved toward an armchair. Josephine stopped him with a look. "Stand inna middle of the room, Sweetie. I wanna see you do a strip."

Da Sallo blushed and walked stiffly to the center of the carpet. The girls waited. At that moment Filo laughed, and the men suddenly noticed faces staring at them through the living-room windows. The Vampires came into the room, several of them curtsying as they crossed the threshold. It was only then that Da Sallo realized who had invaded his home.

Jean-Louis Lombard was feeling both contentment and irritation. It was some time now since he had received his correspondence school diploma in private investigation and been accepted into the detectives' union. Yet in the three months he had been living in town, and despite the fact that he advertised faithfully in *The Independent*, he had had only two clients. Neither case had been particularly challenging. Now, just when he was thinking of moving back to Paris and taking a job in an established agency, trouble was beginning to simmer in the town. That very afternoon seven clients had shown up, a few of them sneaking into his office well after dark. He had even been late for dinner and had had to face his wife's questions and a burned soufflé. What was worse, he had missed the television showing of *The*

Misfits, directed by John Huston, starring Clark Gable and the ineffable Marilyn Monroe. On the other hand, he was two thousand francs richer than this morning. All seven clients had paid him a retainer. When he thought about it, he had no reason to complain.

Lombard dug a spoon into his favorite dessert of meringue covered with whipped cream. The amazing thing was that all seven clients were the target of anonymous letters, and all seven of them were very, very frightened. They had insisted, no, demanded, that he be particularly discrete in his investigation.

Lombard finished the last of the meringue just as his wife brought in his evening cup of decaffeinated coffee. He wiped up a dab of whipped cream with his finger, rose, stretched, groaned comfortably, and sat down in his favorite black vinyl easy chair before lighting up a Celtique 100 cigarette.

Turning off the television he picked up the book on the psychology of anonymous letter-writers he had borrowed from the town library: *Die Psychologie des anonymen Brefschreibers*; in translation, of course.

They made the last transvestite strip while standing on top of the Jaguar. The two men before him had become hysterical and been punched into silence, the girls eagerly joining in the discipline. The frightened men were bloodstained but appeared to be in fairly good shape, all things considered. The Vampires had fallen quiet, seeming a little lost, as if they did not know what to do next. The six homosexuals watched them tensely, wondering what was in store for them.

Luigi Da Sallo was worried about his collection of paintings, especially the Delacroix and two de Staëls. He prayed the Vampires would go before the girl with the razor took it into her head to start slashing the canvases.

A horrible, hairy, stupid Vampire was sitting on the Neupert harpsichord, its fragile legs cracking under his weight.

"How much will it take to make you leave?" Da Sallo asked.

"How much you got?" Freddie demanded.

"I don't know. Whatever is in the safe."

"How much?"

"Twenty-five hundred or three thousand francs."

"Hand it over."

"And you'll leave?"

"We'll see. Hand it over."

Da Sallo found the key in his desk, pushed aside a small Dali etching, and opened the wall safe. He removed 2850 francs and handed them to Freddie, who counted the money before sticking it into his pocket.

One of the Vampires lifted a Ming cup from the glass curio cabinet. The protest died in Da Sallo's throat. The Ming cup soared across the room like a clay pigeon on a skeet range. Da Sallo began to cry.

"Hey, Pops, whatchu cryin' over some damn cup? It don' even have a handle, how you gonna drink outta it?"

Filo slid behind the wheel of the Jaguar, shifted into first, and smashed into a signed Louis XV *secrétaire*. Then he backed out of the room, scraping the Jaguar's left fender as it went through the French doors. Turning on the car's headlights he put the Jaguar through a series of skids across the lawn. Then he opened the car's windows and drove directly into the pool. The Vampires cheered. The Jaguar floated gently in the turquoise water for several seconds, Filo sitting quietly behind the wheel, a withdrawn expression on his face, as if he were meditating. Loud, bubbling sounds came from beneath the car and the Jaguar began to sink.

Filo waited until the car hit bottom, pulled himself through the window, walked to the side of the pool, and climbed up the ladder. Two of the homosexuals had fainted. The Vampires threw their inert bodies into the pool where the shock of cold water revived them.

"Okay, le's get outta here," Freddie said.

"Ladies, you havva nice party," Josephine cooed.

47

The Vampires disappeared into the night. Silence fell over the house, and the lawn suddenly seemed very empty, except for the deeply gouged marks of feet and tires. Bubbles rose from the submerged Jaguar.

After a few moments Puig began to put on his clothes. The others imitated him. "I'll get them," Puig whispered, pulling on his shoes. "I'll get them."

The long drive back to Paris helped settle Puig's nerves. He had memorized the faces of the bastards who had broken into the house and swore to himself that he would get even. One of the men in the back seat could not stop sobbing. The trip to Paris was one long lamentation.

Luigi Da Sallo found some sleeping capsules in his dressing room. He was glad to be alone for a while, glad that François would be gone until morning. Humiliation shared with a loved one is more difficult to forget than humiliation suffered alone.

Da Sallo swallowed a sleeping capsule and then went back into the living room to survey the damage. He could feel the sting and heat of tears filling his eyes. Opening the Louis XV country armoire that held the Fisher stereo, he pulled out an album of songs and madrigals by Monteverdi. Sitting slumped in his favorite easy chair he puffed on a Cuban cigar, feeling his muscles beginning to relax as the cool, classic sound of *Lamento della Ninfa* filled the room.

Outside, in the dark beyond the swimming pool, a man knelt, aiming a Remington repeating rifle. The man held his breath: the barrel steadied.

The bullet entered Da Sallo's head just above the left eyebrow. His body slid to the floor like a puppet whose strings have been cut. The cigar remained clenched in his teeth, the long ash intact.

Later that morning, when François Puig returned, he was greeted by the soft ticking sound of the diamond stylus as it tracked, to and fro, in the album's last groove.

48

CHAPTER

5

It was ten in the morning of Whitsunday and whoever was in charge of the church bells was really hanging in there. Of the town's three Catholic churches, Saint-Just-of-the-Holy-Terror was *the* church, confessional of the town's better families, spiritual home of the upper classes. For the last fifteen minutes parishioners had been entering the church parking lot. They drove only the best: Citroën, Mascrati, Bentley, BMW 3000, and Mercedes of all sorts. There were even a few examples of Detroit iron. It was evident that one simply did not walk to Mass at Saint-Just.

In front of the church, an outstanding example of 1920s exotico-baroque architecture, the faithful greeted each other, smiling in unspoken understanding of their position, aware that they were being watched. The talk was of safaris in Kenya, of the veiled charms of the Orient, or of the latest fad, vacations in Antarctica: two weeks in an overheated Quonset hut, eating real Eskimo Pie. Too divine.

The men were obviously not given to experimentation in their dress. They tended toward a certain rustic sobriety, except for those landowners wearing the suedes and woolens they called "hunting attire." The women, in contrast, were dressed to the teeth. A few of their more anorectic daughters, with voices resembling tweety-birds, wore the red hunting jackets known as "pinks," and black velvet riding helmets.

Father Léon de Bonnefeuilles pressed his eye to the peephole cut in the heavy oak door. The best seats were already filled, the audience was almost ready. He raised his hand. An altar boy flipped a switch and a spotlight began to glow over the altar. Léon de Bonnefeuilles had a sure sense of theater. Forced into competition with television, he had adapted state-of-the-art technology to his own use. His long, lean body, clothed in clouds of incense from the censer, backlit by twin spotlights, was an absolutely Shakespearean sight. Today, the dramatic effect would be further heightened by his red ceremonial robes and the deep tremolo of his trained tenor voice. Leon had star quality.

He opened the oak door and pushed the two small boys ahead of him. The contrast between the tiny children and Léon's own El Grecoish appearance was a sure crowd-pleaser. The church fell silent as he walked toward the altar. He could sense that today was going to be one of his better performances. He had prepared a top-of-the-charts sermon in celebration of the new Japanese amplifier. He'd even pushed the treble a bit, just enough to raise goose bumps and send shivers up his audience's back. Léon pretended to ignore the squeal as the German-made speakers sent feedback to the preamp.

Father de Bonnefeuilles had often played with the idea of lifting the ban on applause after sermons. It galled him to think of the bravos following the concerts held in the sanctuary. He, too, needed an occasional dose of adulation. After all, he was only human.

His most faithful parishioners, a group of thirty-two handpicked society ladies known as "Women United for the Safeguard of Morality," were seated in the first two rows. The dear ladies had invited him to their annual picnic in the woods, directly after Mass. It was therefore even more vital that his sermon move them, that he find some way to touch their rich little souls.

As soon as he reached the altar he began to talk, words racing hell-bent from his mouth. Léon was an ace at sermons, so well-versed in the techniques that he had often considered teaching acting to newly ordained priests. Léon thought of himself as the Orson Welles of the Sacrament. The church ceremony and setting were his own, private *Citizen Kane*.

Leon read from Apostles 2:1-11 with all the virtuoso flair of Horowitz playing Scarlatti. Fabulous.

After the intro, a change of pace, just to prepare the crowd for the dramatic intensity of the sermon to follow. He read the Gospel in a flat, uninflected style, sostenuto and cantabile, deliberately following the metronomic rhythm of Saint John's own words.

The sermon, when it came, lasted seven minutes and thirty-five seconds. He had taken as his subject "Drugs and Violence," and composed a wild, hypnotic chant that had his audience in tears about three minutes into the piece: a new record.

But the true moment of ecstasy came with the Offertory and Communion. Opening the silver box, Léon uncapped the censer and poured in a subtle mixture of two-thirds incense to one-third Bombay Black hashish. One swirl of the censer and his lungs glowed like Pacific coral. God's love slid through his veins. The choir began to shimmer.

The parishioners in the first rows gently fell into an ecstasy of contemplation which they later attributed to the priest's preaching style. The ladies of the WUSM smiled angelically, swept away by the divine fumes, reaching heights of Sabbath bliss they had never known before as they knelt to take Communion.

Léon de Bonnefeuilles jabbed Hosts into the open mouths before him with all the precision and élan of a matador planting banderillas. Alba moved slowly up to the altar rail, holding back, waiting until the last parishioner had taken Communion before kneeling. She wore a long white dress and looked more celestial than ever as she breathed deeply of the fragrant incense. Her eyes gleamed, her expression was as pure and innocent as a babbling brook. Alba recognized the aroma of Bombay Black from having smoked it at school. She took advantage of the free hash as long as she could, wondering all the while what the priest would think of the surprise she had planned for the picnic.

The blade slammed into the tree, vibrating like an arrow from the bow of a Cheyenne warrior. The boy was beginning to get the hang of it, as talented at knife throwing as he was at playing the piano. Gorodish had invited him, along with a dozen of his friends, to spend Sunday at the cabin. He had picked up the children at city hall, after first buying enough food to feed an army.

Gorodish threw the knife. It dug deep into the tree, so deep that the children could not pry it loose. They gathered around as he showed them the proper grip and demonstrated the timing of a throw, the wrist snap, and release.

Taking the pianist aside, Gorodish said: "How would you like to try out for the Paris Conservatory in October?"

"My folks have been talking about hiring a professor from the conservatory to help me prepare for the audition, but it's awful expensive. I'll probably have to work with Miss Oloff again."

"Don't worry about it, kid, I'll take care of everything. But you're going to have to work hard this summer: a lesson every week."

The children gathered around the table and fell on the food Gorodish had bought in town. They ripped apart the chicken, they dug into the mustard, they grabbed at the pickles, and devoured thick slices of buttered bread. They all wanted to come live with him in the woods, no school, knife throwing, all them animals.

Gorodish lit a fire and then opened boxes of chocolate and coffee eclairs, amazed at how much they could eat.

The boy was a true talent. Perhaps he would succeed where Gorodish had failed. Although he had given up his dream of a concert career, music was still a part of his life. He'd never been happier than the day they'd delivered the old upright piano he'd seen advertised in *The Independent.* The felt on its hammers was moth-eaten and the wood full of worm holes, but it could still be played. Gorodish sat down and began the *Concerto Italiano.* Eclairs in hand, the children listened.

In the middle of the second movement, in the midst of an almost religious silence, Gorodish suddenly thought of Alba. He wondered if she liked music.

Jean-Louis Lombard often reassured his clients by telling them that he worked slowly but surely. This time the excuse did not work: his clients were becoming impatient. He had tried to convince them that no progress could be made until he read the anonymous letters. To a man, they had refused his request.

"Please sit down, Detective Lombard," said Commissaire Leblond. "How is your investigation going?"

"I'm not getting anywhere."

"Just be glad you're not in my shoes. They're driving me crazy." Leblond lit a cigarillo. "It's an impossible situation. I'd need ten times more men to cover all the angles, and it doesn't stop. I'm afraid to answer my telephone anymore. I don't have a clue to what's going on, and poor old Judge Bonneau . . . he's been assigned to the case . . . he doesn't know if he's coming or going. The whole town's scared. Streets empty by ten at night. Well, maybe that's a blessing. I don't know how far this insanity can go. People keep trying to tell me it's the heat, the hottest year we've had since 1927. Let's hope the circus will relieve some of the tension. Are you going?"

"I have better things to do. . . ."

"Plassin's article said they've got some wonderful new animals this year. . . ."

Boulou the Clown drove the brightly striped old Cadillac through town. Saga, the trapeze artist, sat next to him, overseeing the music that came blaring through loudspeakers attached to the car's roof. Saga held a microphone to his lips, inviting the townspeople to attend a performance of the world-famous, exciting, death-defying, for-the-first-time-anywhere, one-ring traveling circus.

The town's children had not slept for a week in anticipation of wild animals, monkeys, trained horses. Now most of them were at the sideshow and menagerie, staring at the animals and freaks, admiring the red-and-green wagons that carried the circus through France, marveling at the tent rising in the field outside town. Behind the bars of a cage an elephant swung his trunk. A tethered Peruvian llama stared haughtily at the gawkers.

Chico, three hundred pounds of muscle and the brains of a flea, opened his eyes wide. His eyelids looked as if they had been crotcheted. A noise came from his throat. Twenty years of club fights throughout Europe had left him with a face that appeared to have been sculpted by a bazooka. He had begun his boxing career in arenas where the crowd expected to see the claret flow, and ended his career as a bust-out wrestler. For the last seven years he had worked the circus, sometimes doing a fire-eating act, most of the time playing the strong man, snapping chains, lifting weights, and breaking boards with his bare hands. He was useful to have around, especially when they lifted canvas: he took the place of a winch when they raised the tent.

Chico sat on a chair that at one time had been strong enough to bear his weight but now squeaked each time he sighed. His small, deep-set, dull eyes stared at an item in *The Independent*. Another croak came from his throat. Fanfan, the seventy-eight-year-old roustabout who had shared a trailer with Chico for the last five years, looked up. Fanfan had worn a steel corset ever since the day, forty years before, when he had fallen from the high wire. "What is it, Chico?" Fanfan said. "What're you tryin' to say?"

"Dey crazy in dis place," Chico managed to convey after several attempts. "Looka dis what it say inna news. . . ." He held out the newspaper.

Hungering for virtue and morality, thirty-two female parishioners gathered in the forest glade, to be greeted by the warble and twitter of oh, look at the precious birds. What a marvelous idea, Father (coddling and petting him beyond all propriety), a picnic!

Father de Bonnefeuilles held Alba by the hand. Even though not a member of one of the better families, she had been adopted by the ladies of the WUSM. Delicious, pure, beautiful Alba: in a real sense, her presence helped confirm their self-image. And even the priest, himself, said that the girl was very intelligent.

"Ladies, shall we pause for a brief moment to give thanks for the beautiful day that God, in his infinite goodness, has granted us. . . ."

A chorus of squeals and small hysterical cries greeted the saintly man's words. A blanket was spread on the grass and the priest installed himself in its center, his mind still fuzzy from the sanctifying censer. His admirers surrounded him.

"Father, your sermon was sheer inspiration. What mastery of the language, what oratory, what theological subtlety in your message! I quite felt myself redeemed of my sins! Yet humbled, Father, humbled. You'd be a hit at Notre Dame!"

"Marvelous sermon, Father, and that short passage in Greek: such ease, such maestra, Mary, herself, must have touched you in your cradle. Of course, everyone knows that the De Bonnefeuilles family produces nothing but scholars. . . ."

55

The priest basked in their adulation, their words like balm to his soul. He had watched them take out their lace hankies during the sermon, had seen them delicately wipe tears from their eyes. Léon knew how to play on the female sensibility. He knew how to coax tears from the deepest corners of their souls, to keep them dangling on the tips of their lashes until his golden voice shook them loose to trickle down those richly powdered cheeks. Léon had the gift. Exercising that gift was his greatest pleasure in life.

Alba seemed far away. She sat on the grass, removed from the crowd around the priest. "Isn't she just like a painting by Renoir?" one of the women whispered to her neighbor. "So charming, so delicate, so beautiful. That white dress is perfection!"

The women opened their picnic baskets to reveal finger sandwiches of caviar, thinly sliced ham, turkey, cucumber, watercress, and herbed butter.

Exquisite petits fours wrapped in damask napkins found their way into the priest's hand. They went wonderfully with the champagne. The priest beamed at his ladies, wishing he could find a legitimate reason for holding more of these little outings.

Seated at the edge of the forest under a delicate umbrella of leaves, the ladies daintily stuffed their faces. One of them found the courage to blot at the priest's hand when a slice of tomato happened to soil it. The priest held out his paw to the woman's ministrations, like a bishop allowing his ring to be kissed.

No sooner was the meal over than two boys appeared, carrying two urns of tea that Father de Bonnefeuilles had prepared with his own precious hands. Alba had helped him, the dear girl. The priest's admirers had been led to believe that he was a connoisseur of tea. It was part of his image, a signature of the role he played.

In honor of the day's festivities, he had chosen a mixture of Darjeeling and Earl Grey teas, brewed with a hint of sugar and lime.

The priest served the ladies, pouring the tea into the crystal and silver goblets they had brought especially for this ritual. The tea, and its ceremonial pouring out, were the priest's personal contribution to the afternoon.

Alba glanced at her Bulova Accutron watch. The thirty hits of LSD she had stolen from a schoolyard dealer would soon take effect. She had dissolved the acid in the hot tea while Father de Bonnefeuilles had been slicing limes, his back turned to her.

Heads began to nod, pupils grew as large as grapes. A few women discreetly sponged their foreheads. Could it be the champagne that was making their heads turn so deliciously? The priest began to chuckle, undoubtedly enjoying some metaphysical punch-line known only to him. A few seconds later, the entire group burst out laughing.

A woman held a grass stem in her hand. "It's so beautiful, so beautiful," she murmured in a warm, sensual voice.

Another woman snaked her way across the grass, her body trembling, hissing noises coming from her mouth.

The priest's body was tingling and his eyes felt as if they were popping from his head. Confusedly, he wondered if perhaps he had not used too much Bombay Black in the censer.

"Ladies, ladies, please: a little decorum," a woman cried, desperately trying to hold on to her own self-control.

Alba had not touched the tea. She pretended to stagger as she moved among the women, helping them, goading them on.

One of the ladies removed her blouse, the better to feel the blue-pink wind on her skin. Then she crawled toward the priest, rose to her feet, and held out her hand. Solemnly, the priest stood. Without touching her, he led the woman into a tango. An unsteady dip quickly disintegrated into a game of vroom-vroom-airplane.

A recent convert to Catholicism began to sing a psalm. Three women played leapfrog. Another woman began to cut off a friend's dress, slicing through the waistband with a paring knife, slitting the back of the blouse, the bra strap, the panties. The strippee, her face drawn, stared dumbly at the knife. Alba helped the knife wielder pull the clothes from her friend's body and then moved on as the woman began to caress the naked breasts.

The priest threw himself on a basket of food and happily chewed away. He stopped, overcome by violent hiccups after gorging himself on thirty-five sandwiches. The snake woman wound herself around his legs. Father Léon forced her back down to the ground, reached into the basket, and began covering her with slices of buttered bread.

Another woman climbed a tree, slipped, fell to the ground, and lay motionless. The leapfrogging ladies turned on each other, scratching fiercely with their expensively manicured nails.

Alba moved over to a woman who had recently been busting her chops about purity and virginity, and kicked her in the rump.

A plump woman recited a poem by Mao-Tse-tung, repeating it over and over, like a broken record:

> "Red, orange, yellow, green, blue, indigo, violet,
> Who is dancing, weaving his colored ribbon against the sky?
> The sun returns, slanting after the rain
> And hill and path grow a deeper blue. . . ."

Alba took out her Kodak Instamatic camera and shot three rolls of highly picturesque, fervently pastoral scenes. Then she left, unwilling to waste any more time on the pitiful priest and his flock. She knew that nobody would ever dare mention this particular picnic in the woods.

As night fell, dazed and haggard figures sneaked through the trees, heading for home. Only the priest remained behind, to sleep in the forest until morning.

At six o'clock, dressed more comfortably in jeans and her Indian tunic, Alba arrived for the circus's evening performance. A smell of sawdust and animals filled the air as she took her seat inside the tent. The band began to play, the music bringing tears to her eyes. The ringmaster, in top hat and black riding coat, stepped into the ring, his long body standing out against the ellipses formed by twin blue spotlights.

Gorodish sat among the children he had brought to the circus. Their faces were sticky from the caramel apples he had purchased from a candy butcher.

Trained white horses were followed by a juggler, a wheel of sequined rings rising behind him like a sparkling peacock's tail. Alba loved his hands. They moved so quickly, yet the rings seemed to float slowly around him, the gleaming circles hypnotic as they spun against the dark. When the lights came up again she saw Gorodish seated directly across the ring, talking to a girl. Alba's lips began to tremble. She paled and, for the first time in her life, felt a strange pain in her belly. The man for whom she had invented nightly ceremonies, midnight rites during which her mind left her body and traveled the uncharted heavens, was there, before her. And he cared so little for her, and her beauty, that he dared speak to another woman. Alba wanted to throw him to the lions. She wanted to watch while they ripped and tore and devoured his flesh.

The lights dimmed again. Spangled acrobats climbed up to the trapeze. She strained to see Gorodish's face in the shadows. The music stopped, a drum roll, and the fliers soared gracefully through the air, their costumes glittering. Alba watched the bodies floating above her head in that indeterminate space called "the air," and could no longer feel her own body. Her soul seemed to have fled, to have risen upward toward the twinkling lights.

The Wizard of Constantinople moved slowly toward the center of the ring, dressed in a bright red tunic and diamond-studded turban, his arms held out at his sides as he glided forward, as if born on a flying carpet. The Indianish music accompanying his entrance held Alba spellbound.

When the music stopped, there was a long, impressive silence, and then an amplified voice filled the tent.

"Ladies and gentlemen! For your edification and entertainment, we are honored to present the Wizard of Constantinople! After many years of travel throughout the world and into the deepest heart of India, seeking out the great mysteries of the Orient, the Wizard has only recently returned, bringing with him the greatest feat of magic ever presented in public! Ladies and gentlemen! The man you see before you is no mere illusionist, but a veritable Merlin, imbued with strange and mysterious powers. And as proof that what you are about to see is not a trick and does not rely on wires or lighting effects, but is actually happening before your very eyes, the Wizard asks the cooperation of a young lady from the audience. A young lady from your own town. Is there a young lady present in the audience who would care to volunteer? Is there someone who *dares* join the Wizard in the center of the ring?"

Alba had taken only a few steps before the spotlight found her. The blue-white light followed her down the stairs, carried her across the sawdust, and up onto the red carpet where the Wizard stood waiting. She came to a stop about three feet away from the magician, her body still, yet, somehow, flowing toward him.

Alba tried to see Gorodish in the dark beyond the ring, wanting to touch him, to move him, wanting to use the Wizard as a magic intermediary between them.

She saw the Wizard's dark, bony hands approach her face and felt his fingers pressing against her temples. A slow warmth insinuated itself under her skin, growing ever warmer until it burned like a lava flow. The Wizard's eyes seemed to absorb her soul. The tent was silent. She could feel nothing but the intense heat running through her body.

The Wizard dropped his hands and stepped back. Alba stood immobile, frozen in the cold blue of the spotlight. He moved forward again and touched her lightly. She collapsed in his arms. The Wizard held her tightly, her long blond hair trailing to the floor, revealing the delicate temples and the long, slender neck, as pale as lotus petals.

Slowly, the Wizard raised his arms. Alba lay stretched across his forearms, pale and quiet as death. He closed his eyes and concentrated, her body seemingly weightless in his hands.

The Wizard stepped back until Alba appeared to be supported on only the tips of his fingers. Another moment of concentration. A muted drum roll. The Wizard slid his hands from beneath her body, leaving Alba floating in the air. He backed away a few more steps, lowered his hands, and bowed slightly in response to the applause. The lights went out.

Alba felt an electric shock run through her. She was standing upright on trembling legs, the tent dark, the Wizard's strong hands on her shoulders. "Don't move," he said softly. "Come back, come back into your body. Slowly, now. Breathe deeply."

When the lights came up again she could hear the applause: it had not stopped during the entire period of darkness.

"Come with me," the Wizard said, "you can't go back to your seat yet." She followed him toward the gold-fringed curtain, watching it open before her like the mouth of Ali Baba's cave, then close again, shutting out the applause. The Wizard sat her on a chair, then returned to the ring to take a bow. Two boys worked the ropes that opened and closed the heavy red curtain. Three horses galloped past, carrying rhinestone-clad riders. The Wizard stood before her again.

Gorodish tried to push through the crowd. The curtain opened and three horses came dashing through. He could see Alba sitting just a few feet away.

The Wizard smiled gently at her. "I want to go home," she said. He led her out of the tent.

She was alone, the sounds of the circus faint, seeming very far away. A lion roared nearby and she began to tremble. A steel mesh tunnel next to the lion cages led back toward the main tent. Her hand reached out. A bolt slid back and the gate began to swing open. Alba ran.

A hundred feet down the road she stopped and looked back. A lion was just stepping from the cage.

CHAPTER

6

AFTER WATCHING THE CIRCUS
lion tear three people apart, and searching in vain for Alba,
Gorodish went home and to bed. His sleep was uneasy,
punctuated by brief, hallucinatory dreams in which lion-
mauled bodies melted into Alba's pure, sleek form as it
floated in space. In his dreams he felt her warm and quivering against him, saw her wet, half-parted lips, her breasts,
her smooth abdomen. The music of birds singing inter-
rupted his dreams and he wakened with a sense of loss so
profound that his whole body ached. Desperately, Gorodish
tried to fall asleep again, seeking to reestablish the dream
link to Alba's body, but his mind felt as if it were flooded
with light, leaving him with not even a remnant of a dark
corner in which a dream might be hiding.

He opened the shutters. The forest was bathed in a milky
light and the dew-covered leaves shone strangely. A few
pieces of kindling and three small logs brought the stove to
life. He held out his hands to the crackling wood, trying to
warm himself. Water began to boil in the battered kettle.
Gorodish finished a piece of chicken left over from the chil-

63

dren's party, then brewed a cup of strong tea to which he added three sugar cubes and a dash of milk. He drank. Alba.

The students sat daydreaming, staring out the window at a large oak tree whose leaves shivered in the breeze. Only a few of the more dedicated scholars tortured their brains over an algebra problem, zealously scratching away at their notebooks. Most of them had merely copied down the problem and then stopped: the school year was almost over and they were planning their vacations.

Jeanne Leluc had taught algebra at the *lycée* for the last seven years and was no stranger to these end-of-term doldrums; the torpor and lassitude of the classroom were beginning to affect her, too. She put on her glasses, pursed her lips, and frowned, sweeping the classroom with a gaze as warm as a square root. The dreamers pulled themselves upright in their seats and pretended to work.

"Genevieve, please close the window."

Like a giraffe rising to its feet, a tall, freckled girl unfolded herself from behind a desk and dawdled over to the window.

They're as soft as marshmallows, Jeanne Leluc thought. "Is anybody finished?" she rasped.

Silence. Heads shaking back and forth.

She turned to one of her favorite students, a boy whose eyes seemed unable to focus on anything except numbers. "Roger, are you almost finished?"

He knew she was going to make him go up to the chalkboard and work out the problem in front of the class. In a voice as monotonous as the ticking of a Swiss clock, he said: "Almost, madame."

"Come up to the board, then, and show us. . . ." Roger rose and stumbled up the aisle to the dais, sabotaged by his own ungainly feet and preadolescent awkwardness.

Three minutes later he looked over at Jeanne Leluc, his face red, his eyes filled with terror.

"Has anyone gone further?" Jeanne Leluc asked the class.

Roger took comfort in the dead silence that greeted the question. His complexion returned to its normal yellowish hue.

Imperiously, Jeanne Leluc held out her hand to the fledgling Einstein. He surrendered the chalk and soon the board was covered with letters and numbers.

Something whistled through the air. A dagger planted itself in the wall, six inches from Jeanne Leluc's left ear. The blade was still vibrating when she slid to the floor in a dead faint.

The driver pulled a lever. A winch groaned and the Jaguar rose from the water. François Puig watched the car emerge from the pool and swing down toward the lawn, like a helicopter coming in for a landing. The tow truck dragged the Jaguar away as Puig walked back into the empty house.

Da Sallo had left him the house as well as all his other property, except for a small sum of money meant to support a school for blind children in Italy.

Puig went into the living room and sank into an armchair. Filo's and Josephine's faces were engraved in his memory, haunting him. The police investigation had not even begun: that idiot commissaire was too busy with other things to assign someone to the case.

Puig rang for the maid and ordered champagne and some glasses to be set out. A Citroën DS 21 entered the grounds, drove up the gravel driveway, and parked in the courtyard. Puig went out through the terrace door to greet his visitors. Three unmistakably vicious men walked toward him across the lawn.

Simonetti, Corsica's largest supplier of heroin to the United States, was an old friend of Puig's. He had agreed to help. For a price.

The leader of the group shook Puig's hand and murmured his name. Franco Mutti was rapier thin. A pink scar zigzagged down one tanned cheek and his black hair was slicked back, neo-Valentino style. He wore a suit that looked as if it had been tailored in London.

The two men with him were not particularly bright but they did not need to be. They looked as if nothing short of a jackhammer could stop them.

The men sat down. Puig opened a bottle of Veuve Cliquot. Franco Mutti took a sip and nodded appreciatively before getting down to business. The two button men listened quietly, holding the delicate champagne flutes in their fists, too polite to ask for a beer, or a Coke.

Water soaked the park path, fine droplets carried by the wind drenching the passersby. The afternoon strollers broke stride to avoid the fountain, but Alba stood directly beneath the spray, feeling the drops gliding down her face, watching the rainbow formed by the water as it arched against the sun. When she had had enough she turned and ran, the short skirt swirling around her petal-soft legs. An old man woke from his reverie long enough to see the blur of her passage, then closed his eyes again.

Alba stopped, the wet red shirt clinging to her skin emphasizing the small, heaving breasts. She raised one hand and pushed back her long, blond hair.

A man filmed his wife as she posed beside the fountain. Alba noticed a handbag and another camera on a bench. She glanced at the old man: he was nodding, dreaming of the past. The woman's back was to Alba; the man's eye was screwed into the viewfinder. Alba moved past the bench, slid her hand through the camera strap, and lifted. Holding the camera tightly against her waist she walked on at a leisurely pace until, at last, a stand of trees hid her from the fountain. The man was still shooting pictures of his wife. She broke into a run.

In another section of the park, Alba rummaged through a trash can and found an old newspaper. It was not large enough to cover the 200-mm lens. She found a crumpled paper bag and shoved the camera into it. Then she walked out of the park, moving with the same steady step.

Once in her room she examined the treasure: it was a Pentax ES II fitted with a Takumar lens. She removed the leather carrying case and caressed the bare metal body, loving the feel of it, the weight of it in her hands. The lens seemed to be staring at her. The camera was perfect, just what she needed to photograph Gorodish. A boy at school had taught her how to use a 35-mm camera. He owned his own darkroom and had shown her how to develop film and how to print her own photographs. The boy would do anything she asked, for a kiss.

Filo finished the last of the club sandwich, drank down the rest of the beer, and walked out of the drugstore. Lighting a cigarette, he mounted his chopper. Filo was not very happy. The waiter had been rude. Carefully, Filo analyzed the man's attitude and decided that he'd probably been nervous, knowing he was serving a Vampire. He looked at his watch. It was nine o'clock. He'd promised to see Josephine before the Vampire thing went down later that night and he was late.

Two girls stood watching him; they were a little young for his taste. Filo revved the engine two or three times, ran his hand through his hair, released the clutch, and kicked into first gear. The chopper slid smoothly away from the curb. Filo was careful with his cycle. Racing starts were for geeks who thought they were hot, roaring off on their damn pussy bikes. You just didn't do that to a cold engine.

The black Citroën DS followed the Norton. "This is going to be a snap," said one of the hit men.

"Yeah," said the other, "they didn't need us just to take out that little piece of . . ."

"Shuddup," Franco Mutti suggested. "Puig says he's a tough little bastard, uses a razor. I don't want you leaving any skin behind on this one."

Mimi, the larger of the two men, grunted, signifying doubt. Mimi was the diminutive form of "Mirage," a nickname he had earned because of the rapidity with which he dispatched his victims. He had never yet been seriously wounded during a hit; the only time he had been hurt it had been nothing more than a .22 round in the fatty part of his thigh. Mimi shoved his hamlike hands into his vest pockets and brought out the tools of his trade: two ivory-handled straight razors, heirlooms willed to him by his grandfather who had founded the family business. The carvings on the handles were of museum quality; the blades themselves were so keen they could have split a personality lengthwise. Bebert, the smaller man, was a modernist, an adept of the Chicago school. He used a standard Cobra .38 Special and was so good at his work that he had reached the venerable age of fifty-two unscathed. Not a negligible accomplishment in his line of work.

Julius' darkroom was in a converted tool shed at the far end of the garden. His parents were rich and the darkroom equipment was of professional caliber. Alba found the boy seated in front of the drum dryer. A bare bulb hung from the ceiling.

"Did you bring the camera?" he asked.

"I borrowed it from my father."

"Let's see."

She pulled the camera from a tote bag.

"Too tough! A Pentax ES II! You have the other lenses, too?"

"No. Papa couldn't find them."

"The aperture isn't big enough for night photography; you'll have to push the film. I've been working with some Record 3200 ASA my old man brought from Paris; I've got a few rolls left. But you'll need some light when you shoot. You'd better work with the aperture at 4.5."

"Will you be around tomorrow?" Alba asked.

68

"All day. I have to develop everything I shot last week. You going to come over?"

"Maybe. Maybe I'll have some film to develop."

"You going to shoot tonight? Does your father let you stay out that late?"

"No problem. He thinks I'm sleeping over at a girl-friend's."

"You're lucky. My folks won't let me do anything except my photography."

"You working late tonight?"

"Yes. They don't bother me on Saturdays, just so long's they know I'm in the darkroom. But they're always telling me I'm going to ruin my eyes."

"Listen, maybe I could come back later and we'll print up my stuff?"

"Okay." He hesitated. "You want me to come with you?"

"No. Just wait for me."

"Okay."

Julius turned on the red light and loaded the Pentax, winding the film to the first frame and setting the shutter speed, aperture, and ASA settings. "If you don't have enough light you can set the shutter at one-sixtieth of a second, that ought to do it." He handed her the camera. Alba slipped it back into the tote bag.

She looked so beautiful in the red safety light that Julius could not resist touching her face. She smiled. He held her gently and kissed her on the mouth. Alba leaned against him. Julius kissed well and he was nice, the nicest boy she'd ever fooled around with.

"You wait for me, no matter how late I get back," Alba said.

"I'll be here."

He opened the door and watched Alba disappear into the night. He felt dizzy. But, then, he always felt dizzy after kissing Alba.

Filo parked the cycle in front of Josephine's house. Half a block behind him, the black DS slid over to the curb. When Josephine came out of the house and climbed on the chopper, Mimi let out a whistle.

They followed the Norton out of town and down a small country road. The Norton roared along: there was plenty of time before they had to meet the others at the garage. Josephine pushed Filo's hair to one side and kissed him on the neck.

"Now?" Bebert asked, as the Citroën crept up on the cycle.

"Not yet. We're too close to town."

Josephine felt a strange foreboding. She turned to look back and saw the DS following them, its headlights off. The moon was at last quarter.

"Hey, Filo, there's a car followin' us, no headlights. It's been behin' us ever since we lef' town."

Filo turned and saw the dark shadow of the car against the darker black of the road, a good hundred yards behind them. He cursed, shifted into second and accelerated.

"Hey, boss," Mimi grunted, "they're rabbiting."

"Damn!" Franco downshifted, jammed his foot against the accelerator, and turned on the headlights.

Frightened, Josephine pressed tightly against Filo's back. The Norton's speedometer was wavering at 110 miles per hour as the iodine quartz headlights blazed out across the road. Filo glanced into the side-view mirror. He was about two hundred yards ahead of the DS, but it seemed to be gaining on him. The Norton roared like the Loch Ness monster as Filo strained it to its limit. Their only chance of escape lay ahead, in the hairpin curves still a half mile away. Filo crouched low over the gas tank, Josephine flattening herself against his back and turning to check on the car.

"We're gaining on them, boss," Mimi said.

"That little bastard's got one hell of a motorcycle."

70

"Norton," said Franco Mutti.

Bebert pulled out the Cobra .38 Special and held it against his knee. Filo leaned into the first curve, the throttle full open, the bike bending so low he could feel the foot pedal scraping the ground. Car tires squealed fifty feet behind him as the cycle took the next three curves at a hundred miles per hour.

Franco almost lost it in the first curve and had to downshift to keep from skidding off the road. A small swerve, a tap on the brake, and they were into the second curve, the speedometer holding at seventy.

The road lay straight again. Filo could feel icy sweat running down his back. There was a dirt road ahead: it was their last chance. He downshifted and turned right, the chopper sliding in the mud. Behind them the DS wobbled, its tires shrieking as it spun out and came to rest across the width of the asphalt road. Filo could hear the transmission screech as Franco jammed it into reverse, braked, and slammed into first gear again. The car flew up onto the uneven dirt road, shock absorbers clicking like castanets. Bebert's head hit the roof liner.

Filo stood on the pedals, motocross style, as the cycle flew up the dirt road in second gear.

Mimi and Bebert gripped the door handles, ready to move.

The Norton's front wheel rose up into the air and the cycle flipped over. Filo and Josephine pulled themselves from beneath the wreck.

"He's mine!" Mimi shouted, leaping from the car.

Josephine stood behind Filo, watching the two men spring from the still-moving car. One man stood with his legs spread, his huge body silhouetted against the car's headlights, a gleam of light in each fist. The other man stood to his left, his right arm pointing toward them.

It's so cold out inna country, Josephine thought. Filo charged the man directly in front of him. A terrible burning

71

slash, and it seemed as if his left arm was no longer attached to his body. There was a hole where his left ear had been and a stream of something hot was pouring down his neck. The headlights blinded him as his razor bit into flesh.

Mimi watched a piece of his own neck fly through the air, white in the glare of the headlights. His hand flashed out. There was a cry, and Filo collapsed.

The boy had been blocking the quarter moon. Mimi blinked at the white crescent. Something that felt like a helicopter rotor scythed through his throat, and his arms beat the air. God, I'm dead, he thought as he fell. Just a few more thoughts as he lay on the ground: The bitch, I forgot all about her.

"Don't move, Bebert," Franco shouted, his body crouched in rapid-fire position as he aimed at the girl. "Let go of that letter opener or I'll drop you where you stand!"

Her mind gone blank, Josephine tossed the straight razor into the open field. Then she began to scream.

Franco tapped her skull with his blackjack. She saw a burst of daylight inside her head and the ground seemed to open beneath her feet. She fell.

"Dump the bitch in the backseat," Franco said. "We pump some smack into her, turn her out: she'll make one hell of a hooker."

At one in the morning Gorodish sat at the table in front of the open window, snacking on salami. Hidden behind a chestnut tree sixty feet away, Alba watched him through the camera lens. She loved his face, loved the way he sat framed in the window. She took three more shots and bent to reload her camera. Something cracked in the woods. Instinctively, she held her breath, hearing other, barely perceptible sounds. Three shadows crept out of the woods and entered the small clearing. Alba's heart began to pound so hard she thought it would break through her ribs. Five more shapes came into the clearing. Alba slid to the ground and crawled back into the underbrush, her hands damp and sticking to the cold metal of the camera body. The small house stood surrounded in silence, figures, like dark lizards, clinging to its walls.

Gorodish poured a glass of Beaujolais. He loved these moments of solitude, these solitary, late-night snacks. Something made him put down the glass. Rising from his chair he picked up the fireplace poker, opened the cabin door, and listened intently. Something was out there, in the dark.

"Put down the club, ol' man, we ain't gonna hurtchu." Someone came into the cabin through the window. Then three boys were holding him so tightly he could not move. Gorodish did not even try to struggle as they bound him to a chair with thin nylon cord.

"I suppose you're after my money," Gorodish said calmly.

"You sure don' scare easy, do you, ol' man? You ain't nervous at all."

"I've seen a lot worse than you."

"Yeah, you inna art business."

"If you're after money, it's in the cracker tin, on the mantel."

A girl opened the box. Most of his money was hidden elsewhere in the cabin. Gorodish knew they would never find it.

"Hey, ol' man, we don' wan' your damn grocery money."

They were all inside the cabin now. Alba rose quietly and aimed the camera. The lens was shaking. She slid over to a tree, leaned against it, and shot four frames. Gorodish was being tied to a chair, seven or eight Vampires crowding around him. She saw them press a piece of cotton to Gorodish's face, dosing him with chloroform or ether. She snapped another photograph. Gorodish disappeared from view: they had undoubtedly put him on the bed.

The Vampires came out of the cabin. They got into the

73

Citroën station wagon and drove away, three boys riding on the hood, two others clinging to the luggage rack. The headlights flickered through the forest as the car disappeared. She could hear the Vampires' laughter echoing through the trees.

Alba went into the cabin. Gorodish lay asleep on the bed, the nylon cord slack around his arms. Alba stared at his face, at his closed eyes. She touched his chest. He was breathing easily. She knelt, caressed his forehead, and then bent nearer until she could feel his breath on her skin. Holding his head in her hands, she pressed her mouth against his fleshy lips. Ecstasy filled her.

Alba backed away from Gorodish and snapped two pictures of him asleep. Leaving the cabin door open, she returned to the forest path and retrieved the bicycle she had stolen earlier in town, placing the camera carefully in one of the saddlebags. Opening her blouse to the waist, she could feel the wind against her skin. The deserted road moved beneath the bicycle wheels, the night embracing her body as her soul soared. Ten minutes later she reached town, passing the Danton café, the movie theater, the closed stores. Gorodish's station wagon stood parked at the far end of the street, the sight of it startling her so that she almost fell.

Alba abandoned the bicycle at the curb and, carrying the camera, walked up a side street until she reached a point from which she could see the station wagon clearly. The Citroën stood under a lamppost, casting its shadow against the windows of the Crédit Agricole Savings Bank. The car was empty. Alba moved again, trying to find a better vantage point. A building was going up, directly across from the bank. The fence surrounding the construction site was dotted with signs warning: DANGER. DO NOT ENTER. She found a break in the fence and slid through.

Silence. Water dripping into a barrel. In the dark Alba bumped into the formless objects that filled the construction site, slogging through mud until she reached the foot of a rough staircase. She began to climb, moving up through a skeleton of joists, cement blocks, mounds of sand, piles of brick. As she pulled herself out onto the second-floor landing, her feet crunched on cement grit blown in by the wind. Through a roughed-in window frame she could see the station wagon directly beneath her. Alba snapped a picture and then settled back to wait.

A car passed, then, a little later, a moped. The night was cold and she felt very much alone. Somewhere in the distance a dog howled. She thought of Gorodish, the image of his face superimposing itself on the street below, his amber skin warming the gray damp surrounding her.

She heard a door open, steps, whispers. The sound grew louder. Four Vampires appeared at the corner. Alba lifted the camera and shot a frame, the shutter as loud as an explosion in the silence. The Vampires walked toward the car, carrying a canvas sack. She shot another frame, and another again before they got into the station wagon. The headlights went on, the motor started. She shot one last frame as the car disappeared around the corner.

Suddenly she realized the extent of the favor she was doing for Gorodish while he lay sleeping, unconscious, unknowing. She sat down on a pile of bricks and waited for her heart to stop pounding. After a long while she felt her strength return. Rising, Alba climbed down the unfinished stairs and made her way out of the construction site.

CHAPTER

7

INSIDE THE GARAGE, ITS DOORS firmly shut against the glow of dawn, the Vampires lay sprawled on mattresses and cushions, sinking even further into a deep, depressed silence. It had been such a good plan. There'd even been a chump to take the heat. And now: zip. Only 4500 francs and some paper that looked like stocks. What the hell could they do with stocks? They should have waited until the end of the month, when the bank was filled with payroll money.

To console his friends, Freddie brought out a hundred grams of aluminum-wrapped Afghani Chitral hashish that he'd bought on his last trip to Paris. The Vampires did not waste time rolling joints; they tamped the black, gluey stuff into hash pipes and lit up. A few heavy tokes and the pipes glowed red, hot as steel furnaces. Their disappointment and depression began to melt away.

Everyone was high now. Nerves unknotted. Bodies relaxed. Minds began to wander. One of the girls wondered idly where Filo and Josephine had gone. Then there was no more thought but only clothes coming off, bodies coiling around each other, writhing like snakes in a slow-motion Babylonian orgy accompanied by moans of love and grunts of orgasm.

Gorodish woke around eight in the morning, his head heavy and dull-witted. The open cabin door reminded him of the Vampires' nocturnal visit, but nothing seemed to be missing. The car was outside, although not in its usual spot. The keys were in the ignition. Obviously, the Vampires had gone for a joyride. For a moment it seemed to Gorodish as if he could read their minds, could picture their idiotic little brains operating with all the predictability of programmed robots. Still, it wouldn't hurt to poke around town and see what they had done.

Just before nine, Gorodish pulled up in front of the Danton. Plassin was already there, sipping at his morning glass of white wine. It looked more and more as if Plassin put the paper together at the café, rather than at his office.

"Hail, Balzac!" Gorodish called.

"Morning, Gorodish."

"How're things?"

"Eventful. The Crédit Agricole was burglarized last night. They took forty-five hundred francs and some nonnegotiable bonds."

"My station wagon was stolen last night," Gorodish said. "Maybe I ought to say 'borrowed.' They brought it back this morning."

"Curious."

Gorodish drank a café au lait and ate two croissants before following Plassin up to the offices of *The Independent*.

"I'll just look through my mail and then we'll go report your stolen car to the commissaire." Plassin picked up a large manila envelope and hefted it, noticing that it bore no stamps. He opened the envelope, pulled out the photographs, and spread them across his desk. Plassin began to chant names from the calendar of saints: it was hard to tell if he was cursing or praying. Gorodish glanced over his shoulder and felt himself go pale. For the first time in a long while he almost lost his self-control.

PHOTO 1:   Gorodish eating salami.
PHOTO 2:   Gorodish, tied to a chair, surrounded by
           Vampires.
PHOTO 3:   Gorodish being chloroformed.
PHOTO 4:   Gorodish unconscious on the bed.
PHOTO 5:   The station wagon parked in front of the bank.
PHOTO 6:   Vampires carrying a canvas sack from the bank.
PHOTO 7:   Vampires climbing into the station wagon.
PHOTO 8:   The station wagon driving away.

"Interesting photographs," Plassin said. "Too grainy, though. Hard to get good reproduction on newsprint stock. Looks like Record film, available light, no flash. It must be interesting, having your own official photographer following you around."

As Plassin continued talking Gorodish suddenly realized what had been missing from his plan. The original idea had been too simply stated; it did not leave enough room for improvisation. Now, he rewrote the opening bars of the piece, restating the theme, composing several possible variations, intrigued by the possibilities of the last movement, knowing that tempo was what counted now, determined that it would ring out forte, fortissimo, sforzando.

The commissaire opened the manila envelope. At last somebody had sent him evidence he could use. He did not care who had sent it: this would be the first case to be solved since the beginning of hostilities in the town.

Leblond gave orders for an emergency team to form up in front of the police station. When he came out a few minutes later, he found fifteen heavily armed officers waiting for him. Leblond jumped into the black Peugeot 404 lead car. The police cars started off, a Black Maria bringing up the rear.

Inside the police station, Gorodish and Plassin dictated

statements to the police stenographer. Gorodish signed his deposition and then went to a bakery and bought six croissants. Photography had become a leitmotiv of his plan: he would carry it as far as he could.

Marble entry hall, mirrors, green plants. It was a little early in the morning for this sort of visit, but he had to move quickly now. Seventh floor. Ding (E-flat), dong (G-natural). He leaned on the buzzer. The charming creatures were undoubtedly still humping in the arms of Morpheus.

"What time is it?"

"I've brought croissants, my darlings, and I will even make the coffee."

"Oh, you lovely man! Breakfast in bed!"

The somnolent purrs coming from the blue bedroom mingled with the murmur of boiling water. Gorodish put five heaping soup spoons of pure Brazilian coffee into the paper filter: he wanted them awake. He found the tray, the butter, the milk, the currant jelly, the sugar, the silverware.

A creamy light came filtering through the silk drapes. The little sisters lay nude in the large black bed. Gorodish placed the tray between them, kissed each of them on the forehead, and then lay down across the foot of the bed, leaning on one elbow like a Roman emperor. They complimented him on his artistry, on his subtle tray arrangement, on his manner of serving breakfast in bed.

"You should come see us more often, darling. You're so good at this."

"I've moved out of town. I'm living in the woods now."

"How can camping out compare with all this, darling?"

"It can't, of course; but I'm here on business today."

"Do tell us, darling."

"Do you happen to know Judge Bonneau?"

"We used to, but he hasn't come around lately. With all the scandal in town, the incredible stories we've been hearing, people are afraid to go out at night. Our business has fallen off terribly."

79

"Maybe I can help."

"We knew we could count on you, darling."

"I've heard that you used to be interested in photography, and that you just might have some pictures left. Of Robillard, for instance?"

"Oh, that. We gave it up, darling. Much too complicated. It was simpler to raise our prices than go through all that preparation and lighting and so on. And Robillard is a bastard. That was one case we considered a public service."

"Do you by any chance happen to have Judge Bonneau in your collection?"

They looked at each other and burst out laughing. "He has rather special tastes, darling. Domination. The whip. The whole bit."

"Perfect. How much do you want for the photographs?"

"Why don't you take off your clothes first, darling. We can talk money later."

Led by seven motorcycles, the patrol cars drove up and stopped about five hundred yards from the garage. Armed officers moved forward, crouching in the approved manner, spreading out to encircle the garage. When his men were in position, Leblond came forward, followed by three senior officers. As he neared the garage door, the commissaire pulled out his side arm. It suddenly occurred to him that he had not asked Plassin to cover the arrest. The one time the police were on top of a case and he had forgotten to invite the press.

They slid the garage door open and stepped in, quickly deploying to cover the entire area. When their eyes became accustomed to the dim light they stopped in their tracks and just stared.

It resembled a twelve-headed dragon. Only two or three faces could be seen, moving above the mass of bodies. The mess would have to be untangled before they could arrest anyone.

80

Flushed with frustration, the three officers lowered their weapons. There were some damn good-looking girls in that pile: a real harem. There was a funny, unfamiliar smell in the air, a mixture of body odor, patchouli, and hashish. The mass of bodies was beginning to show signs of reacting to the police presence.

"On your feet!" the commissaire shouted.

Most of the Vampires were still high. It took a good five minutes before they could figure out which hands and feet belonged to whom. The Vampires straggled out of the garage, parading slowly toward the Black Maria as if moving in solemn procession toward a cathedral.

Too bad, thought the officers accompanying Commissaire Leblond. We'll never get a chance to use our weapons outside the firing range.

Gorodish felt as if he were flying. Not only had the sisters screwed him cross-eyed, but they'd also sold him the photos at a reasonable price. He headed for the drugstore. It was three in the afternoon and he was hungry.

He ordered chicken curry, a carafe of Beaujolais, and a Super Vesuvius Fujiyama Sundae topped with currant liqueur. Instead of his usual espresso, he ordered an Irish coffee.

If it hadn't been for those photographs, and for three witnesses who had seen his station wagon parked in front of the bank, Gorodish would have been sitting in a jail cell, waiting to be interrogated.

His lips touched the whipped cream on top of the Irish coffee. And he saw Alba making her way through the restaurant, coming toward him, dressed in jeans and an Indian tunic. He put the glass down and his heart began to pound.

Alba sat down at Gorodish's table as if they had known each other forever. Incredible, he thought.

"Buy me a banana split?"

"Of course."

"I took the photographs."

"With your Instamatic?"

"No. With a Pentax ES II automatic, 200 mm lens, if you must know."

"Not bad." There did not seem to be anything else to say. The waitress took the order.

"What's that you're drinking?"

"Coffee with Irish whiskey and cream."

"May I have a taste?"

Gorodish handed her the glass. Her eyes were as cloudy and mysterious as the background in a painting by Leonardo da Vinci. She held the glass gracefully in one hand as she drank.

"How did you do it?" Gorodish asked.

Alba stared up at him with an unfathomable smile on her lips. The waitress put the banana split down in front of Gorodish. He tasted the vanilla ice cream, the whipped cream, the strawberry topping.

Alba took a long swallow of Irish coffee, the cream leaving a white outline around the furled edge of her upper lip. The tip of her pink tongue erased the frayed white cloud of cream.

"I did it because I'm in love with you."

There was a long silence. Alba pushed the Irish coffee back toward Gorodish and pulled the banana split across the table. "Before I took the last picture, I kissed you."

Gorodish saw a faint flush rising in Alba's cheeks.

"I hid and watched you. I wanted to take a picture of your face, and your hands." She ate a spoonful of ice cream and then looked up at him again. "I'm in love with you because I know everything going on in town is your doing. You're making it all happen. Remember the day you arrived? Remember the train station? The moment I saw you I knew something extraordinary was going to happen."

She finished the ice cream, leaving one banana untouched. "I have to go home now, I'm late. But I could

82

meet you here after school on Monday. I could stay until six in the evening. Okay?"

"I'll be waiting."

Alba pulled Gorodish's left hand across the table and gently pressed her lips against it. Gorodish watched her leave, running lightly down the glass staircase, her blond hair swaying across her back one last time before she disappeared.

Gorodish ordered a cognac.

Commissiare Leblond emptied the evidence bag on the table. They had searched the garage thoroughly, ripping open mattresses, digging up the ground, and even partially demolishing the walls.

The clerk was ready, holding an official form against his chest. The commissaire cleared his throat and began:

"Three hard-core porn magazines."

"One pistol. Semiautomatic. Browning 6.35. With magazine."

"Hash pipes: seven."

"Water pipes, of the type known as 'bongs,': four."

"Ess-and-em photographs, male and female. Looks like some of the Vampires, themselves."

"*The Selected Works of Chairman Mao-Tse-tung.* That's three words: Mao, Tse, tung."

"A cake of hashish, weight forty-seven grams."

"Hypodermic syringes: two."

"Tablets, as yet unidentified. Send them to the lab."

"Cassette tapes of a violent or pornographic nature."

"Nineteen pieces of a dark-brown, transparent substance, each piece measuring a half-inch square."

"Knitting needles used in the manufacture of arrows."

"Straight razors: five."

"Switchblade knives: eight.

"One sawed-off shotgun."

. . .

It was Monday morning. Judge Bonneau stepped from the bath, his skin red from the heat of the water. A smile of satisfaction lit his face as he climbed up on the scale: 257 pounds. The diet was definitely working. Turning sideways, he inspected himself in the mirror, checking the curve of his paunch. Not bad. He'd be able to eat a normal meal today.

The day's business demanded a certain ceremony in his dress. He put on a dark blue suit, a sky-blue shirt and a Bordeaux-colored tie. A gray doeskin vest added a touch of gaiety to the ensemble. His wife had gone shopping. He had asked her to prepare a leg of lamb for lunch: he would be hungry after today's court session.

The maid had left honey toast and coffee on the dining-room table. Perfect. Judge Bonneau had not slept well. Commissaire Leblond had showed up at eleven the night before, bringing along signed confessions from the four gang leaders. Bonneau had no objection to the haste with which the case was being handled. It simply meant that he, too, would have to act quickly. This was one time the press would not be able to claim that justice was being deferred. The perpetrators had no possible defense and he planned to deal with them severely.

He wiped his mouth on a pink napkin. The coffee tasted terrible. He would ask his wife to buy the coffee beans elsewhere.

Bonneau looked at his watch. In less than a half hour the defendants would hear him pronounce sentence on them: two years, with no chance of parole. With all the evidence the police had found, not only drugs, but that vile pornography that was turning the country's youth into monsters of sexual depravity, they were lucky to get off so lightly. And, of course, there were the political implications of the case. . . .

The judge rolled sticky tape across his sleeves. He had bought the lint remover in Switzerland on his last vacation. The Swiss were an ingenious and moral people. He was looking forward to living out his retirement among them.

As he was about to leave, the concierge brought in the morning mail. He thanked her and stepped back into the apartment, placing the letters on the small Henri II table standing in the entryway. A large envelope caught his eye. Curious, he pinched it lightly, then opened the flap.

The Henri II armchair groaned in protest as Bonneau fell into it. His blood pressure rose to 200/140, his mouth as dry as if he had crossed the Gobi Desert on foot. One damp hand touched the knot in his tie, them rose to his left ear as the linkages between his brain and the rest of his body snapped.

Bonneau tried to catch his breath, fanning himself with the envelope. It was then that he saw the letter attached to the photographs:

> Daddykins,
>
> We don't want your money, but our hearts bleed for those sweet, almost completely innocent boys doomed to suffer the horrors of imprisonment for . . . how long were you planning to give them? If you don't want to see the enclosed pictures all over town, we suggest you sentence the poor things to two weeks, just to teach them a lesson.
>
> (*signed*) A good enemy

Commissaire Leblond was waiting at the bottom of the courthouse steps. The two men shook hands.

"Well, Judge, I imagine you're happy with our roundup of the local criminal element?"

"Marvelous, just marvelous."

"You'll be throwing the book at them, I expect?"

"I've been giving it serious thought. As a matter of fact, it kept me awake all night. That is to say, my conscience has been sorely tested by the matter. Justice must be balanced with mercy. Do we have the right to keep these adolescents who may have acted on the spur of the moment, so to speak, from reentering the mainstream and living a normal life alongside other law-abiding young people of their own age? Of course, we must set an example, but once justice has been served we must consider just how many souls are forever lost to society due to the inhumane conditions that reign in our prisons. My conscience will not permit me to inflict such cruel and unusual punishment on these young men. But I assure you, they will not get off scot-free; oh, no, you can trust me on that count. We will make an example of them. I think two weeks is a fair sentence. And let us pray God that this lesson will serve to bring them back to the paths of righteousness."

CHAPTER

8

———

GORODISH SAT WAITING FOR her at the same table. Alba had been afraid that he would not come, that the adventure would go on without her. She would never have forgiven him.

Gorodish stared at her. She was wearing a short-sleeved white cotton dress. As she sat down, she placed a black plastic Nina Ricci handbag on the banquette.

"It's hot today," Alba said. "How are you?"

"What do you want to drink?"

"A double lemon Coke."

"You look as if you've got something cooking. . . ."

"I have a surprise for you."

"What?"

"You'll see, after I drink my Coke."

"Give me a hint."

"You'll have to follow me and just watch what I do."

"Now that we've formed this partnership," Gorodish said, "do you really think that's such a good idea? We have to be careful nobody sees us together. I've been thinking about the two of us and I've come to the conclusion that there's no limit to what we could do, just as long as we're careful. . . ."

"I know you," Alba said, "but you don't know a thing about me, yet. And I still haven't figured out what you're up to here in town. All I know is that the Vampires are in jail, even if it is for only two weeks, and there's a whole lot of people in town fighting in the streets, but you're just sitting back, not doing a thing. It's like you're waiting. And then I show up. You didn't plan on someone like me. . . ."

"Did it ever occur to you that I could change my plans to include you? In fact, it might even turn out better this way."

"How?"

"Patience. We'll be leaving this rotten town, soon."

"You're going to take me with you?"

"Didn't you know I would?"

"I thought we were sort of going to stay around here and squeeze the town dry. . . ."

"You underestimate us. Our combined talents could perform miracles."

Alba instructed Gorodish to follow her at a distance. Tailing her from across the street, Gorodish could not immediately grasp what she had planned for the afternoon's entertainment.

He watched her enter a department store and followed, fifty feet behind.

Alba walked through the store, tacking back and forth through the various departments. There was something different about the way she moved, something feline, and she seemed removed from the noise and activity around her. Alba reached her favorite, the most dangerous, department: Records and Tapes. Ignoring the jazz albums, she headed for the classical records. Gorodish began flipping through stacks of jazz cassettes, keeping well away from Alba. He was delighted that she seemed interested in classical music: it was a good sign. Gorodish began to work his way toward her, curious to see what composer she had chosen. Beethoven. Alba appeared to be comparing various versions of the piano concertos, apparently unable to decide which artist, which interpretation, she preferred. Pulling out an album she glanced questioningly at Gorodish. He shook his head. She pulled out a recording by Alfred Brendel. Gorodish winked. The recording slipped into Alba's black plastic purse. Then, with Gorodish telegraphing his approval, she seized on a four-album collectors' edition of the four Rachmaninoff Piano Concerti, performed by the composer himself.

Gorodish reached for his wallet, preparing to pay. When he looked up, Alba had disappeared. He found her on the other side of the store, in the book department. The girl had style: she was far less innocent than he had thought.

Alba rode up the escalator, Gorodish standing behind her, admiring the long, golden legs, the line of her hips beneath the ecru cotton skirt as graceful as a gazelle.

Gorodish almost tripped over his own feet as the escalator reached the third floor.

A store detective appeared to be observing Alba as she studied the displays of stereo equipment. Gorodish tried to think of some way to warn her. Although the man was standing directly behind her, she did not seem to notice him.

"May I help you?" a salesman asked.

"Do you have portable stereos?" Alba replied.

"Yes. We carry three models. How much do you want to spend?"

"I don't know."

"This model sells for 168 francs. We have another, at 252 francs. And there's our top-of-the-line model, built-in speakers, diamond stylus, digital clock, for 390 francs."

"Too tough! I got 400 francs for my birthday. I'll take it."

"It has a one-year guarantee. Would you like to hear how it sounds?"

At that moment Gorodish realized that the security man was watching him. Realizing that he looked suspicious, Gorodish moved over to a display case and pretended profound interest in turntables. The security man wandered away.

Alba paid for the stereo. The salesman seemed overwhelmingly grateful: he gave her an antistatic cloth, a dust brush, and several heartwarming smiles.

Alba left the store. Gorodish found her waiting for him on the sidewalk, a carton at her feet.

"Where's your car?" she asked.

"Not far from here."

"We ought to lock this up." Gorodish lifted the carton. "You're pretty good," he said. "I was worried for a minute there: a security man was watching you."

"You didn't have to worry. I know all three of them. They work one to a floor, and every once in a while they trade places. And you don't have to worry about my paying for the stereo: it wasn't my money."

Gorodish placed the carton inside the station wagon.

"Can you drive me to church?" Alba said.

"Where?"

"Saint-Just-of-the-Holy-Terror. I've got some business there."

As Gorodish reached to turn on the ignition key, Alba took his hand and placed a rapid kiss on it. "I want you to have the records and stereo," she said, "but on one condition: you have to teach me how to drive."

The car moved away from the curb. Gorodish held Alba's hand. Her skin was warm and soft. For a moment he wondered if he was dreaming. Then her hand tightened on his, removing all doubt.

"Wait for me in the car," she said, "I won't be more than five minutes. I have to see the priest about something."

She pulled the records from her black purse and left them

90

on the seat, winking at Gorodish before getting out of the car. He watched her walk across the parking lot to the church and push open the ugly door leading to the vestry. Four minutes and thirty seconds later, she was back.

"Guess how much I just made?" Alba said.

"How much was there in the poor box?"

"Don't tease, that stuff's for amateurs: chewing gum on a string. I just made ten big ones."

"This I have to hear. . . ."

"Simple," Alba said, pulling a handful of photographs from her purse and spreading them across the car seat.

Gorodish thumbed through a series of delightful pastoral scenes shot during the course of a genteel parish picnic. His laughter filled the car.

"You really love photography, don't you?"

"Not bad for an Instamatic, hunh?"

"You didn't dry your prints carefully: there are white spots on the finish."

"The priest didn't seem to think there was anything wrong with them. I thought he'd die. God, the man's stupid. He wanted me to give him the prints. I had to explain to him about negatives."

"How did you get them to perform?"

"LSD. You ever drop acid?"

"No."

"I'll steal some at school. We'll trip together, okay?"

"If you like. Now, does this priest of yours have the money?"

"Not yet, but he's going to pass the collection plate. He'll have it by tomorrow night. His ladies are loaded. Maybe I should have asked for more. Do you think I should go back and ask for thirty thousand?"

"It's late," Gorodish said, "six o'clock."

"Oh, I have to get home and make dinner. I haven't had time to shop. Oh, well, they'll eat sardines again and like it. Listen, I won't be able to see you tomorrow, not unless you

91

want to come with me to collect from the priest, around seven o'clock."

"I'll meet you in front of the drugstore," Gorodish said.

"I can take all of Wednesday off," Alba said.

"Why not come to my house?"

"Oh, too tough!"

"Madame will be down in just a moment, Father. Won't you go into the pink drawing room?"

Léon de Bonnefeuilles was in no humor to notice the antiques on display in the small sitting room. How could such a sweet charming child lower herself to blackmail? And how could he go about broaching the subject of payment to ladies who undoubtedly had already conveniently forgotten that moment of abandon?

He heard footsteps and quickly removed an ecclesiastical index finger from his nostril.

He was beginning his quest for donations with the wealthiest of his admirers, hoping that her generosity would allow him to avoid the embarrassment of further interviews. A high, carved door opened and she appeared, dressed in a white silk robe that swept the shining parquet floor.

"Father, how nice, I was not expecting your visit. May I offer you a cup of tea?"

He bowed, feeling himself grow pale. "My dear madame, I have come to you on a matter of some delicacy . . . uh, I don't quite know where to begin. . . ."

"Please, Father, there must be no embarrassment, no hesitation between friends. . . ."

"Madame, do you recall a certain picnic . . ."

"Unh-oh." She sat down, her face turning white under the layer of pink powder. She tried to speak, stammered, stuttered, gathering her courage to say: "I should have thought, Father, that you would have had the tact, the decency, never to mention that obscene . . ."

"Believe me, it is with the greatest embarrassment, the greatest reluctance, that I . . . that I am forced to. . . ."

"Father, I think you had better explain. . . ."

"Blackmail, madame. Last night I was shown certain rather explicit photographs. The blackmailer demands the sum of ten thousand francs in exchange for the negatives."

"But that's blasphemous! The honor of the Church, the honor of its most faithful followers, is being threatened. . . ."

"I've managed to set aside a small sum of money over the years, my life savings, madame; but I fear it adds up to no more than three thousand francs. Believe me, I would have done anything to spare you this unpleasant conversation. . . ."

"But, Father, why come to me? If memory serves, I was not the worst sinner among the ladies that afternoon. . . ."

"Just so, just so, madame, but your past generosity led me to hope . . ."

"Come, come, Father, you know I do not keep that sort of cash on hand. I have five or six thousand francs at most, from my household accounts. You certainly don't expect me to write the blackmailer a check, do you?"

Alba threw the peas into a pot. Her older sister was not home and her father expected his lunch to be ready at noon sharp. She looked at the kitchen clock: 12:10. Luckily, her two brothers ate at the school cafeteria. Alba did not like being alone with her father. From 12:30 on, his already violent temper tended to worsen. Right now he was probably still at the corner bar, downing his fifth *pastis*. Hoping to sweeten his humor, Alba had bought a bottle of good Bordeaux wine instead of the family's usual rotgut. The door opened.

"Hello, Papa."

"Hello. Nobody else home for lunch?"

"Solange went to the dentist."

"Oh, yeah, I forgot."

He sat down at the table and noticed the bottle of Bordeaux. His eyes lit up. "Hey, a decent wine for a change."

93

"How do you want your steak?"

"Rare."

Smoke filled the kitchen. Alba opened a window.

"We don't spend much time together anymore," her father said.

"I suppose . . ."

"I'm glad we have this time alone," he said. "I think we should talk about your future. Do you ever think about what you're going to do with your life? Do you know where you want to serve your apprenticeship?"

"Apprenticeship? Papa, you know I want to graduate from the *lycée*."

"What for? You're smart enough to make it without all that damn education. It's only meant for idiots and rich folk anyway. Listen, I don't bring in enough money on my own to keep this family going. You're going to have to start contributing something, like your sister does. Paul and Simon, well, they've got years ahead of them before they can start bringing in some money. You know, you're not a bad-looking girl. You'll find a husband easy enough. Finishing *lycée* doesn't mean a thing. . . ."

He filled his wineglass for the third time, his voice growing louder. "I'm not made of money, and prices're going up all the time. I'm sick of supporting this family. . . ."

"Okay, calm down," Alba said. "I'll think about it."

"I've got a buddy, head of personnel at that factory where they make those scientific instruments. I could talk to him, I mean later, when you reach legal age and can quit school. There're engineers working there, guys'd make good husbands. A girl like you'll have no problem finding herself a man. Not like your sister, can't find herself a husband . . . when I think she coulda been married for the last two years and all she meets are bums!"

"Did you bring *The Independent*?"

"Sure. It's got all the details about the burglary. What's this town coming to, I ask you? Only a month ago it was a quiet, decent place to live. Now we're turning into America, into New York. A man isn't safe in his own . . ."

Gorodish and Plassin sat in the sun in front of the Danton. Plassin opened the latest issue of *The Independent* and handed it to Gorodish. A headline on the front page read:

WHO PHOTOGRAPHED THE BURGLARY?

The photographs were not clear, but public interest in the story was so high that clarity no longer mattered. The edition had sold out. Plassin had also managed to fill the paper with more copy than usual, including an editorial in a box on the second page with which he intended to clear his friend's name, once and for all.

WHO IS SERGE GORODISH?

Known and respected by the leading citizens of our town, this well-known artist recently became the target of local gangsters seeking to use him for their own ends. In the process they caused suspicion to fall on him for acts they, themselves, committed. After stealing his car and using it to perpetrate their heinous crime, this same gang of criminals produced witnesses to perjure themselves as to Monsieur Gorodish's whereabouts at the time of the crime. Meanwhile, these criminals have been holding vile and lascivious orgies in the garage that, until recently, served as their headquarters.

Fortunately, Serge Gorodish's innocence has never been in doubt. Publication by *The Independent* of the mysterious photographs (see page 1) sent by an anonymous eyewitness has only added to public acknowledgment of his innocence.

But who is this man, this artist, this newcomer who has become the pride of our town?

Serge Gorodish is a man who appreciates beauty, but one who does not limit his love of art to mere contemplation of beauty in its myriad forms. Gorodish is that most rare of beings: a Renaissance man. He paints, he draws, he plays the piano. The children of our town were the first to appreciate, and adopt, this remarkable artist as one of their own. The feelings of love and respect our children have for Serge Gorodish are largely reciprocated.

We were not surprised, therefore, to learn lately that Serge Gorodish is also a philanthropist. During the annual piano recital presented by our well-known Children's Conservatory, Serge Gorodish discovered a pupil trained by Miss Christine Oloff. Thanks to Serge Gorodish's generosity, this town's most talented young pianist faces a bright future on the concert stage. We only hope that Serge Gorodish can forget the unhappy events of the last few days and remember only that we are proud to welcome a man of his caliber among us.

Gorodish put down his glass. "You overdid it," he said. "Every parent in town is going to want me to pay for his brat's education."

"It was necessary," Plassin said. He was as sensitive to the undercurrents of public opinion as Gorodish was to the presence of young talent.

When he finally reached the solitude of his cabin, Gorodish sat quietly for a few minutes in the Citroën, thinking of Alba. He smiled. He was carrying the ten thousand francs she had extorted from the priest; she had not dared keep the money at home.

Gorodish went into the cabin and lit the kerosene lamps. The girl was audacious, incredibly daring. They had spent last evening discussing her family problems. The first step in ridding her of her father was a simple matter of psychological conditioning: Alba was to make sure her father read Plassin's editorial. After that, one visit would suffice.

Gorodish cooked three eggs, over easy, and some bacon. He ate half a *baguette* and drank three cups of tea.

After dinner he set up the stereo and removed the cellophane seal from around the albums, trying to decide which he would listen to before going to sleep. Finally, he chose a Beethoven sonata, Opus 106, played by Brendel. As the first measures rang through the cabin, his soul began to soar. Tomorrow, at eleven, he would see Alba. They would spend the entire day together.

At the very edge of sleep he remembered Alba's pale temples, the fine blue veins, the adolescent hairline, and the first kiss he had pressed against her skin. The scent of her hair perfumed his dreams.

CHAPTER

9

GORODISH WAITED IN THE CAR. he did not see Alba coming until she opened the door and slid in beside him. "Sorry I'm late but I had to work on my father. I got him to read the article about you, sort of setting him up for tonight. He knows you're coming. You're going to have to be really careful, how you handle him."

"Don't worry," Gorodish said. "I'm good with parents."

"Do you think he'll agree?"

"Of course. But even if he doesn't, I'll find some way for us to stay together."

"Are we going to your place?"

"Yes. I bought things for lunch."

"Did you buy some wine?"

"I didn't know you drank wine."

"I don't, but I'd like to try it."

"I listened to one of your records last night. The stereo works beautifully, and you're an angel. . . ."

Alba had placed a large bag on the backseat. "What's that?" Gorodish asked.

"Some of my loot. I'd like you to keep it for me. I always

lock my bedroom door whenever I go out, but when my father gets drunk he can't stand anything getting in his way. I'm afraid someday he's going to break into my room, so I got a lot of the stuff out of there. Listen, I told him you'd be coming over around eight, is that okay?"

"Yes, and don't worry; I know exactly what to say."

It was strange, seeing Alba move around the cabin so confidently, as if they had been together for years. He opened the window. She set her bag of treasures on the table and smiled up at him. He was amazed at the extraordinary atmosphere of complicity, of unspoken understanding, that had sprung up so quickly between them.

"I want you to take anything you like," she said, pulling merchandise from the bag. There were two Omega wristwatches, a Tissot, a Bulova Accutron, a Patek Phillipe, and several less expensive brands. And three Dupont lighters, a Dunhill, a Braun electronic, as well as two table-size designer models. And piles of pens, Shaeffer, Parker, Waterman, Pelikan, Montblanc. And a Niso S 560 Super-8 movie camera, two portable tape decks, ties, leather goods of all sorts, two meerschaum pipes, a crocodile handbag, a Malay kris, an eighteenth-century miniature, a pair of candlesticks, a cardboard box filled with rings, and scores of necklaces, bracelets, a microscope, bottles of perfume, gold and silver compacts, and cigarette cases.

"I just brought the prettiest stuff," Alba said. "There's lots more at home."

"Did you ever get caught?"

"Yes, the first time I tried shoplifting. I stole a chocolate bar and a man saw me. It turned out okay: he let me go. But I made up my mind it'd never happen again, so I practiced and practiced until I learned how to do it, you know, like a scientific system for stealing, and nobody's ever caught me since. But it's getting boring, stealing all these little things. I want to steal something big! A car, maybe, or a bus, a train, planes, boats . . . something enormous. That's why I want to learn to drive."

"Have you ever thought of stealing the Eiffel Tower?" Gorodish asked dryly.

"I'm not a mechanic," Alba said indignantly. "It's got all those nuts and bolts and stuff to unscrew."

Gorodish fingered the objects on the table, unable to choose among the treasures. Finally, he removed the drugstore watch on his wrist and put on the Patek Phillipe. Alba took off her own Bulova Accutron and strapped on the watch Gorodish had just discarded. Laughing, they shoved the plunder back into the bag.

"Are you hungry?"

"Starved!" Alba said. "Can I open the wine?"

Facing each other across the table, they touched glasses before sipping at the Fleurie. Gorodish had bought a *pâté en croûte, foie gras,* salad, and a strawberry tart for dessert.

"All my most favorite things!" Alba said.

"If you want me to teach you how to drive, you'd better drink only one glass of wine," Gorodish warned.

"Can we do it this afternoon?"

"Right after lunch."

"Too tough!" Alba exclaimed, clapping her hands. She stared deep into Gorodish's eyes, managing to devour her lunch at the same time. He could not eat but sat watching her, thinking of the future, picturing it as a long, sunlit road filled with mad escapades and laughter.

Alba plunged her fork into a large chunk of pâté and held it out to Gorodish. "Aren't you hungry?" she asked. Her mouth was red with strawberry juice and she licked her lips with the tip of her pink tongue.

"I was so jealous when the guys told me you'd taught them how to throw a knife and you didn't even invite me. But I really don't care, you know. It's better this way. I don't want to share you with a lot of other people. I want to be alone with you, like we are now. I think about you all the time, day and night, even in my dreams. How long does it take to learn to throw a knife really well?"

100

"It depends what you mean by 'really well,' and how many hours a day you practice."

"I mean enough to kill somebody."

"A few months. You want to kill someone?"

"Yes, especially if I could do it with a knife. It isn't the same thing if you just shoot them with a rifle or something. For instance, if you don't manage to convince my father, I'll kill you. . . ."

The sun shone white through the hot somnolent forest. Alba was wearing jeans and a light blouse. They climbed into the station wagon and Gorodish moved the seat forward.

"This is the ignition. That's it. Now, the parking brake. Okay. Step on the clutch and shift into first. . . ." Gorodish held Alba's hand, guiding her through the four forward gears and reverse.

"That's it, you shift into first. . . . Now press down on the accelerator. Gently! Not too much, that's it. Okay, now let up on the clutch, slowly, slowly. Steer! Okay, go ahead, just don't hit any trees."

The car bucked a few times, the engine hiccuping and then steadying. Alba was tense. She gnawed at her bottom lip and sat stiffly, clinging to the steering wheel. Gorodish could see her nipples jutting out. The sun flickered down through the masses of dense foliage above them, the light playing on the small points peeping through her blouse.

"That's it, clutch, shift into second. Here, let me help you. . . ."

The station wagon glided through the woods with only an occasional jolt when Alba could not avoid a rock or a hole in the forest floor. They reached a crossing of two paths and Alba turned the steering wheel with all the ease of someone who had been driving for years.

"Can I shift into third?"

"No. You don't want to go any faster until we hit a paved road."

A rabbit dashed in front of the car. Alba jammed on the brakes, forgetting to step on the clutch. The car stalled, but she started up again with no help from Gorodish. The car moved on, doing a steady thirty-five miles an hour along the twisting dirt road.

A cloud of dust rose up behind them, hung for a few moments in the hot summer air, and then slowly descended in a heavy cloud that hovered over the forest floor.

"I love driving! Listen, school's over next week. Can I come over every day and practice driving? You'll let me, won't you?"

She turned to look at Gorodish and the car angled off the road and up onto an embankment. Gorodish grabbed the wheel and eased the car back onto the path. Alba glanced from the road to Gorodish and then back again. She resembled an actress doing a car-driving scene, the forest moving in rear projection behind her as she exchanged long, languorous glances with her costar.

She still did not throw the knife hard enough. It hit the tree and fell to the ground, the weight of its handle pulling it free.

"That's better, you're getting it now. The movement's almost perfect, but you have to throw it as if you're aiming for the tree behind your target. That's the only way you'll get some real power into it. And you're hesitating. There's this little hitch in your wrist action just before you let go. Your arm and hand have to work together, in one long, smooth flowing movement. Like this."

Gorodish threw the knife. It planted itself so deeply into the tree that Alba could not pull it out.

"Pay attention to how you open your hand. Not too early, not too late. A clean movement, like this." He demonstrated again.

"Do you trust me?" Alba asked. "Would you stand in front of a target and let me throw knives all around you, like they do in the sideshow?"

"You'd have to be a lot better at it than you are now," Gorodish said. "The way you throw, the blade wouldn't go in very far, but if you hit in the wrong place, you could do some real damage."

Alba laughed and launched herself at Gorodish, punching him on the shoulder. "Want to fight?" she whispered passionately.

Gorodish put his hands on her waist and raised her until their faces were even. Then he pulled her toward him and let her slide down the length of his body. Small drops of sweat stood at her temples and just beneath her lower lip. He wiped her temples with the palm of his hand, his fingers burying themselves in her silken hair. She leaned against him, her blue eyes staring deep into his own.

"Would *you* let me throw knives at your pretty little blond head?" Gorodish laughed.

Alba tore herself from his embrace and ran to a tree, standing in front of it with her arms held out at her sides, as she had seen the human target do in the circus sideshow.

Gorodish bent over and pulled the knife from the ground. He concentrated. His arm rose slowly. Alba closed her eyes, her stomach suddenly feeling empty. The blade thudded into the tree a foot above her head. Alba opened her eyes. Her legs felt a little weak, but she was proud of having taken Gorodish's dare.

They went back to the cabin and listened to the Rachmaninoff Third Piano Concerto. Alba had never liked classical music but she instinctively understood its importance to Gorodish and remained absolutely still until the concerto was over. It was beautiful.

Gorodish bent over to lift the tone arm from the record. Alba could see his scalp through the close-cropped hair.

103

"Maybe you ought to dress up a little when you go see my father," Alba said. "He's impressed by good clothes. You're supposed to be a philanthropist. Those guys wear expensive suits, don't they? And your hair's dirty. Would you like me to wash it for you?"

Shirtless, Gorodish sat on the grass, a bath towel draped around his neck. Alba filled a pan at the kitchen tap and wet down his hair, pouring handfuls of the freezing water over his head. She soaped him gently, her slim fingers sliding over his hair.

"The soap won't lather because your hair's too short," she said. "Maybe you ought to let it grow a little longer. . . ."

"I like it this way," Gorodish said. "It's less bother. . . ."

"I wouldn't mind spending time on your hair. . . ." She soaped his head, her fingers slipping into his ears. "You have such big ears!" she said.

"The better to hear you with, my dear."

"And, Grandma, what a big mouth you have. . . ."

The sun shone through the thin cotton tunic, rendering it almost transparent. He saw the line of her hips beneath the material, sensed the ellipse of her abdomen.

"The better to eat you with, my dear." Gorodish lifted the tunic and bit the soft belly pressed against his face. Alba cried out and jumped back. Her fingers were white with lather. Laughing, she rubbed the spot Gorodish had bitten with a protective, foamy hand.

"You really are a wolf! Next time you try that I'll get soap in your eyes!"

Gorodish grabbed her by the hips and pulled her toward him. She knelt before him, her hands soaping his head, rubbing his neck, sliding down to his shoulders. Her entire body seemed to be smiling.

"What a lovely mouth you have, Grandma."

Gorodish pressed his lips against hers, feeling Alba's soap-slick hands gliding the length of his arms. Her mouth was sweet and vibrant, as aromatic as a lotus.

. . .

Alba's father and Gorodish sat in the living room. Alba's father raised his glass in a formal gesture before downing the contents in a single gulp. Gorodish took a genteel sip of the port and then set the glass aside. "Alba is one of the most gifted children I have ever run across. Remarkable intelligence. You agree, do you not, monsieur, that she could go far, given the chance? . . ."

"Oh, yes, I agree. She always was at the head of her class and didn't even have to work very hard at it, but, you understand, monsieur, since my wife left I've had a hard time supporting my family. My wife earned more than I do. . . ."

"No disgrace in that. . . ."

"No, of course not, and my older daughter does the best she can. But, as the saying goes, Alba's inherited the brains in the family. In two years she'll be able to quit school and find a job. With her brains, she won't have any trouble finding work."

"Monsieur, I do not waste my time on children who can merely find a job. I am only interested in children of talent and imagination, children with original minds. And Alba is one of those rare . . ."

"Very flattering, monsieur, very flattering that you've taken an interest in her. I read all about how you're helping that piano player; they say he's studying in Paris . . . but as far as Alba's concerned . . ."

"My dear sir, that young man's family is also in a difficult financial situation. But they've found they can manage quite nicely with the thousand francs a month stipend I send them. . . ."

"Oh, I didn't realize, of course . . . evidently . . . it's not that I don't want my girl to have the best education she can . . . of course, if she's up to it, it'd be nice if she had an interesting career. . . ."

"If it would make things easier for your family, monsieur, I might be able to pay you the same monthly stipend as the other family. . . ."

"Monsieur . . ."

"With the sole proviso that I take full charge of your daughter's intellectual development and education. She must leave for Paris immediately. In cases like this one must aim high: the best schools, the best instructors. If one waits too long the imagination atrophies, the mind becomes set in its ways, and it is too late. . . ."

"Oh, absolutely, monsieur, I agree. . . ."

Unable to sleep, Alba lay on her bed. Gorodish had pulled it off: he was going to take her with him. She did not know when they would leave but she knew it would be soon, very soon. Her mind was racing. She tried to imagine what her new life would be, stretching her powers of invention to the limit, forming pictures in her mind and then erasing them only to begin all over again, creating new universes, each succeeding one different from the one that came before. Now that she was to be with Gorodish, anything was possible.

She thought of his mouth. His mouth was wide and warm. And there was something else about him, a hardness, a coolness, that she adored. She could feel the sweat on her body and got out of bed. It still seemed a miracle that they were free, free to do as they wished, go where they wanted, answering to no one. All her father seemed to care about was the monthly check Gorodish had promised him.

Alba thought of the town, of the people she knew, of the life she had lived until now. Everything about the place in which she had grown up seemed mediocre and dull. She wished they could leave right now, that she could get into the station wagon with Gorodish and just go, leaving everything behind.

Naked, Alba sat on the windowsill, dangling her legs out over the street below. The warm night air caressed her body.

He had won. Gorodish danced around the darkened cabin. The moment of culmination was approaching, the lines of his carefully composed plan were converging. Everything had been planned down to the microsecond. Twelve more days and he would reap the harvest.

He did not want to think of what would happen afterward. It was a waste of energy, worrying about afterward.

Fully clothed, Gorodish threw himself on the bed. He slept.

CHAPTER

10

THE VAMPIRES GATHERED IN front of the gates, waiting for the four martyrs to appear. Four riderless choppers gleamed in newly waxed splendor, awaiting the hands, and boots, of their owners.

Nobody spoke. Filo's death, and Josephine's disappearance, had shaken the bikers. The Vampires seemed to have lost their energy: they appeared nervous and humbled. Everything had changed since the day the cops broke in and arrested the entire gang. The Vampires had thought themselves masters of the town; that four of their number could be sent to prison seemed a sign of moral bankruptcy and of a decay of power. The atmosphere at the garage was very depressing.

One of the girls kept rubbing a rag over the cycles, polishing the gas tanks. At least they'd kept the choppers in good shape.

Heat and silence of midday. Depression. Chain smoking.

Steps approached. A small door set in the heavy iron gate opened and, one by one, four more victims of police brutality appeared. They looked like whipped dogs. Catching sight of the waiting bikers, they tried to smile, tried to hold themselves proudly. They were bald, their heads shaved. And they'd been beaten. Their faces above the suddenly oversized leather jackets looked swollen and bruised.

The four ex-cons mounted their cycles. Girls climbed on behind them. The other choppers backfired a last, farted insult at the forbidding prison walls. The pack rode up the street and then turned back, choppers roaring defiance as they passed the prison.

"Okay, Monsieur Gorodish, your car's ready. Greased, oil change, headlights and brakes adjusted. You needed a new battery, so I put one in."

"Good."

"All ready for the highway, Monsieur Gorodish. Is it true you're leaving for good?"

"Yes. I'm going back to Paris. It's become too dangerous around here."

"And this used to be such a quiet town. But that was before you came. . . ."

"No, it was very nice at the beginning, when I first arrived. . . ."

"That motorcycle gang's ruined the place. I don't know how you feel about it, but they ought to put people like that in prison and throw away the key. You know the proverb: as the twig is bent . . . Did you hear they got out today? Believe me, nobody's very happy about it. Two weeks! Nothing but a slap on the wrist. It's not going to do any good. Everybody's worried. . . ."

"That's why I'm leaving. You've probably heard they seem to have it in for me. . . ."

"If it was me, I'd be leaving, too."

Gorodish paid the mechanic and headed for the center of town to pick up Alba. News of his departure had spread like wildfire and the townspeople seemed ashamed and genuinely sorry to see him go. Plassin's articles had helped instill them with a profound sense of guilt, and Gorodish's last shopping trip had been gratifying: the baker had given him a coffee eclair, the wine merchant had offered him a free bottle of wine.

Gorodish tried to think of whom he should see, besides Plassin. The editor was one of the only really good people in town. Gorodish admitted to himself that without Plassin's unwitting help his task would have been far more difficult. Gorodish passed many acquaintances as he drove up the Rue de Gaulle, some of them familiar to him only by their presence in his sketch pad and notebook. Each face was the key ingredient in a story, part of the large mosaic he had managed to fit together. Gorodish parked in front of the Danton and went inside for one last *panaché*. He could feel everyone watching as he stood at the bar.

"Sorry you're leaving," the bartender said. "You've become part of this town. People around here don't take easily to strangers, but we've gotten used to you, I guess."

"I'm sorry to have to leave. I liked it here."

Gorodish had deliberately chosen this time of day for his farewell appearance. The commissaire was due to arrive for his morning glass of white wine and Gorodish wanted to bid him good-bye in public.

"So!" Leblond said, "the rumor is true. You're leaving tonight?"

"Yes, unfortunately. But who knows, perhaps I shall be back someday. In a few years . . ."

"May I offer you a bon voyage drink?"

"I'd like that, thank you."

"You must know I'll sleep better at night, knowing that you're safely away from here," Leblond said. "You've probably heard that they were released from prison this morning. Just between the two of us, I'm afraid they'll try to get back at you, despite the fact that you were only indirectly involved in their being arrested. But, you know how it is, that kind of criminal mind has no sense of logic. . . ."

Alba's entire family was waiting for Gorodish to arrive. Even though she was taking only a few personal items, both her valise and a large tote bag were packed. The family stood around her, as immobile and rigid as pawns on a chessboard. Gorodish joined her father in one last toast. The father shed a few tears, as did the brothers. Gorodish promised that Alba would come to visit in a few months, after she was well settled in a proper school and her new life was established. Her father fondled three months' allowance that Gorodish had tucked into his jacket pocket: the windfall helped temper his grief.

They walked in procession to the station wagon. The bag and valise were carefully placed in the backseat. Tears in her eyes, Alba kissed everyone. She could feel delight rising within her and was almost overcome by a rapturous sense of adventure. Gorodish shook the father's hand a long time. After all, he owed the man *something* in exchange for his daughter.

The garage had not looked the same since the day the cops almost destroyed it. The Vampires would have to find new headquarters: it seemed an almost impossible task.

But they had managed to replenish their stock of Moroccan grass. The most recent victims of an outdated and inhumane prison system lolled on cushions, gratefully accepting the joints passed to them. The worst part of their two weeks in prison had been the lack of women. They wondered how inmates serving longer sentences managed without going crazy.

Everybody was high. The girls went to work, trying to erase the memory of two weeks of celibacy. The feeling of depression began to lift.

Afterward, they sat around talking. One piece of bad luck wasn't enough to break the Vampire spirit. The first thing was to take vengeance for Filo's death, the second thing was to find Josephine. It was obvious that Puig had killed Filo, or had him killed. They should have offed him that night, when they had the chance. But it wasn't too late: they'd take care of that faggot.

A touchy sense of honor and a knee-jerk desire for vengeance were two of the bonds that held the Vampires together.

Gorodish and Alba dined with Plassin. The editor found it very hard to say good-bye.

Around 11:30 P.M., Gorodish parked near the cabin and began to load bags and valises into the car. He had promised the gamekeeper he would leave the keys in the door. Alba went through the cabin, checking to see that they left nothing behind. Gorodish picked up the last bag, the one holding Alba's most treasured secrets.

"Let's go," he said.

"Just a minute; I want to show you something."

"We have to hurry."

"Two minutes. . . ."

"Okay."

Carrying the bag Alba walked past the car and disappeared into the dark at the edge of the clearing.

"Are you running away?" Gorodish called.

"Don't be silly. Wait until I tell you, then turn on the headlights."

Gorodish sat nervously behind the wheel, trying to catch sight of Alba in the dark. The night was filled with thousands of small sounds. He wondered what she was planning and felt tempted to call her back but restrained himself. After all, he would have to get used to her caprices.

"Okay! Turn on the headlights!"

The lights pierced a wide, yellow corridor in the night. She stood in front of the quivering trees, her arms lifted toward the night sky, her white body rising like a flower from the black stockings. The satin garter belt and bra traced geometric designs on her skin. Gorodish stared, as if gazing at an apparition. Slowly, Alba began to turn, her arms weaving, her legs barely moving. He did not know where to look first, confused by the sight of long legs gliding through the dark, the whiteness of a belly, the curve of hips and shoulders disappearing into the shadows only to reappear again. Alba stepped back out of the light. The performance was over. Gorodish turned out the headlights.

He heard her coming across the grass. She was dressed again, wearing a very short skirt and a blouse open to her waist. Alba got into the car and threw the bag into the backseat. She slid into Gorodish's arms and they kissed wildly, his hands hard on Alba's waist. He could feel the muscles under the delicate skin straining toward him. Alba spoke, her lips pressed against his, the words losing themselves within Gorodish's open mouth. "Did you like it?"

"Very much."

"I'll do it anytime you want, as long as you want. There's more. . . ." She pulled a red silk scarf from her bag and thrust it at him. "Smell," she ordered.

Gorodish plunged his face into the scarf. A wild, sweet perfume filled his nostrils and his senses reeled.

"Every time I did it, I thought of you," Alba said. "I want you to wear the scarf. Put it on." Gorodish wound the fragrant silk around his throat. "You haven't told me where we're going," Alba said.

"Not far. It's a surprise."

"Do you think of me as a grown-up woman?"

"Oh, much worse than that."

As they drove through the sleeping town they crossed the Vampires. Gorodish felt a chill run up his back. Then he relaxed. He could see they had more important things on their minds.

. . .

François Puig stood in the living room, dressed in his bathrobe. He heard the sound of motorcycles and realized he had only a few seconds in which to save his life. He took a step toward the telephone, hesitated, took a step toward the desk where a 7.65 automatic was hidden, hesitated again, then started toward the French doors, intending to lock them.

A Kawasaki 750 cc blocked his way. The other choppers drove into the room and surrounded Puig, the bikers smiling hellishly as they circled him. When the cycles stopped, a deep silence fell on the room. Puig began to shake.

"Hey, lady, whatchu doin' home all alone?"

Puig could not answer. His throat was tight with fear.

"We jus' wanna know wha's happened to Josephine. You know, Filo's ol' lady, the guy you had killed?"

"It wasn't me," Puig said. "I had nothing to do with it."

"Hey, we don't blame you; we know you wouldn't hurt a fly."

"Believe me," Puig said, "I had nothing to do with it. . . ."

"We wanna name an' address a the guys who did it. . . ."

"All I know is what I read in the newspaper. . . ."

"He's shinin' us on. . . ."

"I assure you . . ."

"You're a stubborn bitch ain'tchu?"

They tied Puig to the harpsichord and cut his clothes away, their razors occasionally biting into his skin. His teeth chattered like castanets as blood seeped from a few of the deeper cuts in his skin.

They did not have to do much more. Puig gave them the name and address.

"He's a nice lady. You been real cooperative, lady, so we gonna make it easy for you. . . ."

"Make it easy?"

"We're gonna kill you. But we'll do it quick. Don' worry, it won' hurt."

"Listen," Puig said desperately, "we can work this out. I've got a lot of . . ."

"You're jus' wastin' your breath. . . ."

The flames rose in the night, the fire reflecting in the turquoise water of the swimming pool. When they were sure that he was dead, the Vampires left. Filo was avenged. That left Josephine. They'd find her. Maybe.

The car moved quickly through the night. Alba slept, her head pressed against Gorodish's shoulder. From time to time her hand moved up to touch his face, his hair. He listened to her quiet breathing and asked himself if he had ever before felt such contentment. After a moment's thought he said "No" out loud. And that was all.

His footsteps muffled by a moth-eaten red carpet, Gorodish carried Alba up the stairs and placed her on the bed. Her face turned away from him in her sleep, the blond hair fanning out across the pillow. Her left hand opened slowly and then closed again as Gorodish pulled the blanket down to the foot of the bed.

Carefully rolling Alba to one side, he unhooked her short skirt. She whimpered but did not waken. Perplexed, Gorodish studied her for a moment and then knelt on the bed to pull off her sandals.

He worked the skirt down over her legs, then unbuttoned the blouse, lifting Alba's inert body to slide her arms out of the sleeves. Carefully, he placed the discarded clothing on a chair next to the bed and turned back to contemplate the uncooperative, sleeping figure. Outside, in the dark, crickets chirped. Gorodish unhooked the stockings. Alba's hand reached down and touched his fingers, an almost imperceptible smile on her lips. He turned her over to unhook the brassiere, her body heavy in his hands. She moaned, then moaned again when he slipped the panties off. He placed his

lips against her knees, against the scant blond triangle, the
dark points of her breasts, and against the wide, pale forehead showing through the fall of golden hair. He watched
the small breasts rise and fall in rhythm with her slow
breathing, then pulled the blanket up around her shoulders
and quietly left the room.

Downstairs, Gorodish opened the top drawer of a console
standing in the entrance hall, removed a set of car keys, and
left the darkened house. A few moments later came the
sound of an ignition whining, followed by the cough of a
long-unused engine starting up. The sound settled into a
steady throb which slowly moved away from the house and
faded into the night.

CHAPTER

11

No TRAINS WERE DUE UNTIL morning and the parking lot in front of the station appeared empty. Suddenly, there was a faint squealing sound. It seemed to come from a midnight-blue Renault-4 parked at the far side of the lot, its color making it invisible in the dark.

The driver, Paul Ribon, yawned, stretched, and looked at the glowing dial of his wrist alarm. It was three in the morning. The watch had cost him a fortune, relatively speaking, but it was the only way he had found to do his job properly. Without the watch he would have slept through until morning.

Ribon had been hired as night watchman by the town's banks. The bank owners, made nervous by the recent burglary attempt, had been very specific about his duties: he was expected to make continuous rounds, checking each of the banks in turn, making sure they were secure. It was not the sort of job Ribon would have chosen for himself, but as a former Nazi collaborator, work had been hard to find for the last thirty-five years.

Ribon had worked out a simple system. He made his first round at 11:00 P.M., checking all three banks, even getting out of his car to try the doors and shine his flashlight through the bank windows. Then he drove to the parking lot for a two-hour nap. His second round came at one in the morning and was even easier: the town was asleep and there was no reason for him to get out of the car.

It was time for his third round of the night. The R-4 wheezed, the engine reluctant to start. The stoplight next to the station blinked yellow. Ribon slowed as he passed the first bank, the Banque Nationale Populaire. A little farther on was the Crédit Lyonnais, and, past that, the Crédit Agricole.

Funny, there was a station wagon parked in front of the Crédit Agricole. He tried to remember back to his last round. There had been no green Peugeot 504 parked there. Well, it probably wasn't important. Nobody would be stupid enough to break into the same bank twice in one month.

"Maybe I ought to check on it. . . ."

Ribon double-parked the Renault, walked back down the street to the green station wagon, and looked inside. It was empty. Ribon went over to the main door of the bank and shone the flashlight on the doorknob. It was locked. His hand let go of the .38 Police Special. He had never used a gun in his life, but his employers insisted he carry one, especially now, at the end of the month, when the banks received fresh shipments of funds.

A noise startled him. It seemed to be coming from inside the bank. The venetian blinds were closed and he could not see in. He remembered a side door and went around the building, pulling the gun from its holster as he approached it. His hand reached for the doorknob. The door opened. Something long and thin entered his heart. He died.

A man ran to the station wagon, carrying four large bags.

· · ·

118

It was 4:10 A.M. The patrol car drove slowly down the Rue de Gaulle. The men inside were not used to night duty but, with everything that had happened in town . . .

"There's not even one café open all night," one of the cops grumbled. "It's inhuman, especially on nights like this. . . ."

"We're lucky. We can sleep days when everyone else is working . . ."

"Maybe you can, but not me. My damn stomach wakes me up at eleven every morning. My mealtimes are all screwed up and I'm hungry all the time. . . ."

"Smoke a cigarette; that'll cut your appetite."

"Where're you going on vacation this year?"

"Peru. The wife and I've been talking about it for years. . . ."

"We're going camping. Nothing like being out in the fresh air, and it doesn't cost . . ."

"What about the camping equipment?"

"Sure, but that's a onetime deal. You make an investment, see, and you use it over and over. . . ."

"I'm going to take my camera along. There're Indians and everything. I'm going to bring back a lot of slides. My wife's giving me a slide projector for Christmas, I already told her what kind to get. You and the wife can come over some evening and watch. . . ."

"You sure there're Indians?"

"It says so in the brochure."

"I thought they lived on reservations."

"No, that's in America. They're not the same kind of Indians. These are good ones, not cannibals. Some of them are even Catholic and they can go wherever they want. . . ."

"I don't like foreign countries. I don't like the food. I went to England once, to bring back my daughter, she was studying English. Well, they raise a hell of a lot of chickens in England but all they eat are the eggs. You'd think they'd try a little chicken in cream sauce once in a while, but they don't know the first thing about good cooking. And you should see what they drink. . . . You can't find anything except beer. . . ."

"Hey, did you see that? The new watchman's car. What the hell's it doing there?"

"Can you figure them, hiring a watchman? They're just trying to take our jobs. . . ."

"Maybe we ought to take a look. . . ."

The glass of Vichy water spilled, knocked over by the commissaire's hand as he reached for the telephone. What idiot was calling at this hour, just as he was about to capture Al Capone? Three years' worth of investigation shot to hell. . . .

"H'lo," the commissaire mumbled.

"Hello."

"I'm listening!"

"Commissiare . . ."

"Fauchard, what the hell are you doing? I told you not to call me for any reason! Do you know what time it is?"

"The bank's been hit. And the watchman's dead. . . ."

"Which bank?"

"Crédit Agricole."

"Don't touch a thing, I'll be right there!"

By the time the commissaire arrived, a group of people had gathered. They parted to make way for him. The medical examiner was leaning over the body.

"Well?" Leblond demanded.

"Very strange. He was killed by a knitting needle through the heart."

"What?"

"A knitting needle."

Something clicked in the commissaire's memory. The evidence taken from the garage, the arrows made of knitting needles.

"The Vampires! By God, this time they've asked for it!"

The car screeched to a halt in front of the police station. Ten minutes later, two cars crammed with police were headed for the garage. This time even the commissaire was armed with a submachine gun.

None of the Vampires could sleep. They sat around, talking about everything that had happened over the last few weeks. Freddie went out to take a leak. He heard two cars drive up, their tires and brakes sounding like the twenty-four hours at Le Mans.

"Cops!" Freddie shouted and took off. Two girls and another biker followed him as he headed for the woods.

Cops jumped from still-rolling cars. A BSA 550 flew past them, right under their noses.

"Fire, goddamit!" the commissaire shrieked, letting fly with his submachine gun.

The girl on the BSA was jolted from the cycle, her spine severed. The boy followed her down, dead before he hit the ground. At that moment two bikers came out of the garage. A dozen machine guns spit flame in their direction, the bullets entering their bodies like a flight of angry bumblebees.

The other Vampires were getting away. The police aimed their weapons in the general direction of the forest and let loose.

Paolo climbed over a fence. Death sank a hand into his intestines and pulled. Paolo gave a small cry and died, his body balanced on the top fence rail.

Thirty feet ahead of Paolo, Jeff turned. The forest was only a few steps away but it was too late. He saw flashlights coming toward him in the dark and thought of war films he had seen. Giant searchlights piercing the sky, searching for enemy planes. An explosion, flak in the left engine. Cannon fire stitching across the plane, the aluminum tearing on the dotted line. Flames. Mayday, Mayday. He jettisoned the canopy. The airplane was in a dive. He jumped clear and floated down through the night. The parachute harness was

121

too tight, painful, across his chest. The ground came up more quickly than he had thought. He rolled, gathering in the silken shrouds. He was in an unfamiliar country. It was death.

"Good morning, Madame Comine."

"Good morning, Monsieur Gorodish. It's good to have you home. When did you get back?"

"Last night, I've been thinking of taking a rest; you know how hectic things can get. Well, the village seems the same as ever."

"Oh, nothing ever changes here. Although we do have three new babies."

"What does that make now? One hundred twenty seven?"

"Monsieur Gorodish, what an amazing memory you have. What would you like this morning? I've stopped baking the all-butter croissants. They've become much too expensive."

"I'll take six plain croissants."

"The country air's given you a good appetite, Monsieur Gorodish."

"I'm not alone; I've brought my ward with me. I'm seeing to her studies these days. You'll meet her soon. Sweet little thing. I'm sure you'll like her."

"You're always so generous, Monsieur Gorodish. The Chastin family blesses you for what you did for their son. Did you know he's found a job with an architect in Paris?"

"Really? He's doing even better than I had hoped."

"We've been reading articles about you in the newspaper, Monsieur Gorodish. We're all very proud of you."

"Oh? I didn't realize that regional paper was distributed here."

"Oh, yes, we're not all that cut off from the outside world. Cherries are in season now, Monsieur Gorodish. Would you like me to bake you a pie?"

"I'd like that. And could you ask Maria to come tomorrow? The house could stand a cleaning."

"She'll be glad to. A big house like that needs to be taken care of. Did you see the Lebanon cedar? It caught some sort of blight this spring but we managed to save it."

"I'm glad. If it weren't for the cedar, I'd sell the house."

"Oh, Monsieur Gorodish, you're always joking!"

The house was set in a garden about five minutes' drive from the village. It was not beautiful but it was secluded and an enormous Lebanon cedar grew in front of it. Gorodish drove through the gate and up the dirt road, parking in the small courtyard in front of the house. The lawn was high and needed mowing.

The shutters were closed and the house smelled of damp. Gorodish opened the French doors that led out onto the terrace. A small, green, wrought-iron table and four chairs stood just inside the living room. He moved them outside. Gorodish loved eating breakfast on the terrace, taking the morning air, and admiring his cedar tree.

He went into the kitchen and looked through the pantry. Luckily, Maria had bought coffee beans. The refrigerator hummed loudly; it had been purchased secondhand. Gorodish put a kettle on the stove and began to prepare breakfast. It was eight-thirty in the morning. The house was quiet. He gave one last glance at the terrace table. It was ready. The front of the house was warming up, the sun's rays filtering down through the cedar tree at an angle.

Gorodish went into the living room. It looked like an antique store, filled with an incredible jumble of furniture, a bit of everything from beautiful country cabinets to Venetian mirrors. He loved auctions and could never resist buying whatever caught his eye. The sight of sunlight dappling the dust-laden furniture suddenly made him feel absurdly happy.

And there was his Erard grand piano, an incredible instrument, especially in the lower register. He played the opening bars of a Bach partita, then went upstairs to Alba.

She lay as he had left her, the red blanket pulled down around her waist. It must have been too hot during the night. Gorodish pulled the drapes and opened the shutters. Going to an armoire he took out a silky turquoise robe he had bought in an American boutique in Paris, and placed it on the bed. The robe looked a little large for Alba, but the color was perfect for her. Gorodish bent down to kiss her, then changed his mind. He went back downstairs. An old bell hung at the front of the house. He rang it vigorously, three times.

Alba opened her eyes. The sheets were of an inhabitual smoothness. Her hand ran up her body as she stared at the high ceiling. Through an open window she could see the top of a tall cedar tree. The room was furnished with an armoire, a dressing table, and a gilt-framed mirror. An open door led out of the room. She yawned, sat up in bed, and rubbed her eyes.

The last thing she remembered clearly was riding in the car with Gorodish. She looked at her watch: 9:05. The place did not look like a hotel. Suddenly feeling lost in the enormous bed, Alba rose and slipped into the robe. She had never before felt anything that soft against her skin. Putting on her sandals, she walked over to a closed door, opened it, and entered a bathroom. Wondering where Gorodish was, Alba splashed cool water on her face and quickly brushed her hair.

Next door to her bedroom was another, larger room, similar to the one in which she had wakened. The morning sun streamed into the room and the bed looked as if it had been slept in. Alba could hear the sound of wind in the trees. She explored the rest of the second floor, discovering two smaller bedrooms and a darkroom.

The red staircase runner was worn. She walked noiselessly down the stairs and through a large entry hall. A library stood on one side of the hallway. She followed the smell of fresh coffee into a kitchen. The odd collection of furniture in the adjoining living room convinced her that she was in Gorodish's house. Then she saw him, sitting at a table on the terrace, laughing as he watched her explore.

"So Her Highness is finally awake."

Laughing, Alba ran out onto the terrace and threw herself into his arms.

"Are we going to stay here?"

"For a while."

"It's wonderful! It's so quiet, as if there were no people for miles around."

"Well, not quite, but almost."

"I love it!"

"I've brought you some croissants for breakfast."

"I've never been so hungry in my whole life!"

Alba pressed herself against Gorodish, feeling like a grown-up woman, picturing herself as the mistress of a slightly crazy but absolutely wonderful man. She buried her head against Gorodish's chest and ran her hand through his hair.

"I almost woke up last night," Alba said, "when you carried me up the stairs. But I didn't want to wake up all the way. It was wonderful, like I was watching myself dreaming. I felt your mouth, and then I fell all the way asleep."

Gorodish handed her a croissant and poured hot coffee into the cups.

"Don't you have any banana Nesquik?"

"No."

"Isn't it strange? We don't know any of those things yet, like how much sugar we take in our coffee or what we like, all that. . . ." She dunked her croissant in the coffee. Gorodish did the same. They began to laugh.

"You own this house, don't you?"

"Yes."

"It's very pretty."

"No, it isn't; the tree just makes it seem that way."

125

"That's strange, too: it's the first thing I saw when I woke up."

"That's why I put you to sleep in that room."

"Isn't there anybody else here?"

"No, nobody."

"Whose car is that?"

"Mine."

"We have two cars?"

"Yes, but that one's worth a fortune."

"What are you talking about? It's just an old station wagon."

"Yes, but there are 950,000 francs in it."

Alba choked on her croissant. Gorodish slapped her on the back, trying to help her stop coughing. "You left me alone last night?"

"Just for a little while."

Alba stared at the Peugeot station wagon. "We're not going to stay out here in the country too long, are we?"

"I thought you liked it here, the peace and quiet."

"I've got a few ideas about how I want to spend the immediate future," she said. "Three days of mad, passionate lovemaking, then three days of sleep, then we take off for Paris. I'll steal a Rolls-Royce, we make the rounds of the high fashion houses, then we rob the Banque de France."

Gorodish rose, kissed Alba's shoulder, and embraced her tightly.

"Have you ever considered getting a vasectomy?" Alba asked seriously.

"Not really," Gorodish replied.

"You ought to think about it," Alba said. "I'm not thrilled at the idea of you getting me pregnant."

"There's no hurry," Gorodish said.

"I've got a lot of things to learn. The sooner I begin, the better."

"Okay," Gorodish said, dragging Alba into the house. "Your first lesson: how to play the piano."

126

MORE ABOUT PENGUINS, PELICANS
AND PUFFINS

For further information about books available from Penguins please write to Dept EP, Penguin Books Ltd, Harmondsworth, Middlesex UB7 ODA.

In the U.S.A.: For a complete list of books available from Penguins in the United States write to Dept DG, Penguin Books, 299 Murray Hill Parkway, East Rutherford, New Jersey 07073.

In Canada: For a complete list of books available from Penguins in Canada write to Penguin Books Canada Ltd, 2801 John Street, Markham, Ontario L3R 1B4.

In Australia: For a complete list of books available from Penguins in Australia write to the Marketing Department, Penguin Books Australia Ltd, P.O. Box 257, Ringwood, Victoria 3134.

In New Zealand: For a complete list of books available from Penguins in New Zealand write to the Marketing Department, Penguin Books (N.Z.) Ltd, P.O. Box 4019, Auckland 10.

In India: For a complete list of books available from Penguins in India write to Penguin Overseas Ltd, 706 Eros Apartments, 56 Nehru Place, New Delhi 110019.